MW00873376

What people are saying about...
Should I Choose to Die Again

After reading *Should I Choose to Die Again*, I am now fully invested in the Hamal books! Lauren Stinton has expertly crafted a narrative featuring engaging characters, such as the healer, Hamal, and the seer, Cale, within a fascinating and unique world I can't wait to get back into. I highly recommend this book—a satisfying plot with enough twists and turns to keep you on your toes.

— Catherine Posey, PhD
www.bookish-illuminations.com

From the opening sentence, Lauren Stinton draws her audience into an extraordinary world of seers and sages, healers and prophets in her latest novel, *Should I Choose to Die Again*. Readers from age ten to adult will find themselves enchanted as Stinton's lovely story of life unfolds in a world quite different from our own—and yet perhaps not so very different at all. Hope prevails in this fantastic world of mystery and intrigue. Stinton's work is reminiscent of both C.S. Lewis and J.R.R. Tolkien in many ways. A delightful yarn for readers both young and old. Highly recommended.

— Jane and Steve Lambert, author and publisher
Five in a Row curriculum

Lauren Stinton has built a vibrant and viable world where the innate natures and callings of people are given cultural and fantastical expression. Personally, I found the story to be very relatable and I'm eagerly waiting for more to come.

— Jim Driscoll, author of *The Modern Seer*

Should I Choose to Die Again is an engaging and enthralling novel about Hamal, who at first appears to be young, simple, and benign. As the book progresses, so does the main character. He not only is able to protect himself in a world of escalating dangers, but he saves and protects others. He has many hidden talents that unfold as the story progresses. I can see my students becoming engrossed in this tale, gaining strength from the main character's resilience, as well as perhaps looking at others with new eyes, realizing that the people around them may have hidden talents that just haven't had a chance to come to light. I look forward to the sequel!

— Robin C. Harbour, teacher
Nelson Avenue Middle School
Oroville, California

SHOULD I CHOOSE TO DIE AGAIN

For Brooke and Kevin

Other books by Lauren Stinton

The House of Elah
The House of Elah: The Alusian's Quest

SHOULD I CHOOSE TO DIE AGAIN

A HAMAL NOVEL BY
LAUREN STINTON

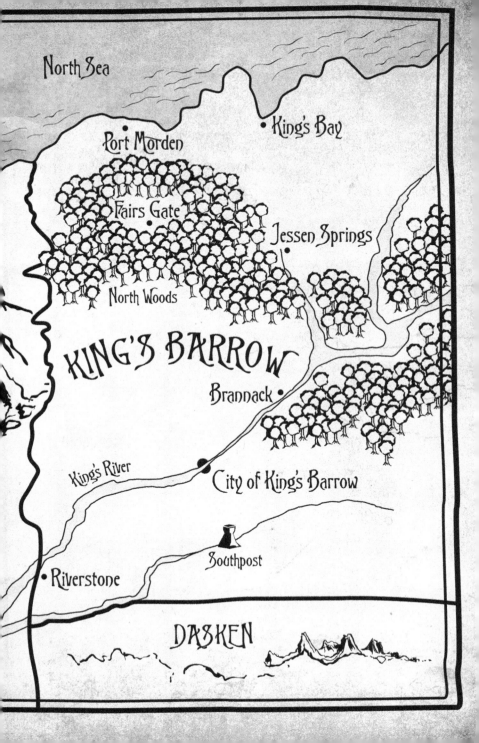

Table of Contents

1 The Dead Man in the Street

Hamal was cold, and he didn't like it. It snowed in King's Barrow every winter, but this wasn't normal, all this white on the ground.

It had been snowing since last night, which he spent in the Kladis Tunnel beneath Scarlet Road. The flamemakers liked the tunnel, so it was usually warm down there, even when it snowed. It had been warm last night, and it would be warm again tonight—as long as the flamemakers still claimed the territory. You never knew what would happen in South Barrow. Nothing ever stayed in the same hands because of all the fighting.

The flamemakers fought with the weathermakers, and the jewelers fought with everybody. Jewelers needed goals, and when nothing good presented itself, they sometimes chose bad goals just for something to do. Sometimes the Kladis Tunnel was a battle-field, and those were the dangerous nights, because the king's soldiers would come to put down the riots. They would arrest every person they could get their hands on. Hamal had lost a few friends that way. One was killed after he landed a solid punch on a soldier's jawline. Another time, two of Hamal's friends—Rinny and Fen, both flamemakers—had taken off into the night, running as fast as they could, which wasn't very fast at all apparently, because they had ended up facedown on the ground as the soldiers beat the resistance out of them.

Hamal was lucky that night. He had reached the tunnel a couple of hours after he normally did, and by then, the soldiers had already broken up the fighting. Hamal crouched down and watched as about a dozen men were chained hand and foot, tossed in the back of a heavy wagon with bars over it, and taken across the river, where they would be sold. Hamal heard that flamemakers were in high demand across the river. He didn't know if the rumor was true, but it seemed true.

Some men preferred slavery to street living, but that was only the case if you had a good master. Some masters made street living look simple and easy. Hamal had heard horrible stories from men who used to work for masters who made them suffer for things that didn't seem important.

Hamal had had a master once—a good man named Richart. Though they had started off as master and servant, Richart had become Hamal's closest friend. He had taken good care of Hamal for ten years, but then he died and Hamal hadn't been able to save him. Richart's son had been angry, so very angry. Hamal still shuddered when he remembered how they had found Richart's body and how the son had responded, demanding that Hamal heal him.

But Richart was dead. He had been dead for hours.

So Hamal lived on the streets now, but he didn't mind. The men typically liked him, and there were many benefits to living with flamemakers, the warmth being one. He could put up with hunger much more than cold. There wasn't much he could do about the cold, because he wasn't a flamemaker—or a weathermaker. Weathermakers were crazy. They didn't even notice when it snowed, and they seemed to think about ice the way they thought about flowers. It was a thing of beauty to them.

He pulled his coat tight about him. At least he had a coat. And he had boots, too, though the toes were wearing out, and there were holes in the heels. But at least he had them. You were thankful for any kind of boots in crazy weather like this. He hunkered down as the wind picked up and blew snow ghosts across the street. That was what he called them—clouds of snow, driven off the drifts by the wind.

Hamal was hurrying, and his head was down, and the wind was blowing, so he didn't see the coach until he nearly ran into the back of it. He stopped so fast that his boots skidded through the snow, and he wobbled, arms flailing, to get his balance. As he righted himself, he stared at the back of the coach and reached up to rub his bare head in confusion. The night sky was thick with clouds and the lighting along the street was poor, but he knew that emblem on the back of the coach. He couldn't remember the name of the family now, but Richart, his old friend, had made him memorize the emblems of all the lords of the king's court.

"You never know when you will need this information," he had said, tapping the side of his nose. He always did that. Whenever he gave instructions, Richart would tap the side of his nose, as if that were the source of his words. "One can never be too careful in North Barrow. We have our own kind of thief here."

What was a North Barrow coach doing in South Barrow at this hour of the night? And it was snowing besides. The driver must be very lost.

The people in North Barrow were wealthy and powerful—the king lived in North Barrow. East Barrow, meanwhile, was home to merchants and other working-class men; all the shipping yards were in East Barrow. West Barrow was the scholars' district. Richart used to say that in West Barrow, you couldn't toss a rock without hitting a student or a school. The nation itself was called King's Barrow, and this was the city of King's Barrow, the city of the king, and everyone was proud of it.

If this coach truly was lost—and of course it had to be; why else would it be here? Perhaps they would offer Hamal a coin to give them directions. He had been paid for such small jobs before. People who lived in the other barrows rarely entered South Barrow, the poor district. There were few jobs here and few businesses that offered anything of value to the wealthy, so it was almost a guarantee that if any of the rich folk did enter the barrow, they would eventually need to stop and ask for directions.

He was about to walk around the coach to talk to the driver, when the door on the right-hand side opened, and a man was tossed out onto the street. He hit the snow with a deep groan, the kind of groan Hamal was familiar with—a teeth-grinding noise of intense pain.

Two men jumped out of the coach after him. They were wearing armor, Hamal thought, but it wasn't the armor of the king's soldiers. The king's men didn't wear black armor; they wore polished silver armor that was so clean and bright that you could see it even at night. These men would have been like shadows but for the snow on the street.

One of them carried a large hammer. The other had a drawn sword. The man in the snow was moving a little, but only a little. Hamal could hear each breath the man took. He had fluid in his lungs. He had been badly injured.

The soldier with the hammer murmured something to his companion with the sword, and they both laughed. The man with the sword crouched beside the injured man on the street.

"You want a message, my lord? You are the message." He then straightened up and put the tip of his blade through the fallen man's chest. It was a very sharp weapon, or the soldier was very strong; either way, the blade passed through the chest without any sign of resistance until it hit the street on the other side.

The dead man's hand came up and almost seemed to caress the blade. Then his arm flopped back into the snow and was still.

For a moment, Hamal didn't know what to do. Part of his brain told him that these men were worse than the king's soldiers. Another part told him to hold still and maybe they wouldn't see him. The snow played with people's eyes. Sometimes, it hid things that otherwise would have been visible. He realized his hands were shaking, but he thought it was probably from the cold. It was very cold out here, and the dead man was lying on his back in the snow—that could not be pleasant for him.

The man with the hammer turned and saw Hamal. The hammer lifted. "You there."

Hamal swallowed hard.

"Yes, you. Tell everyone you see that *this* is what happens when the House of Kanyan is defied."

Hamal suddenly remembered the name that went with the emblem on the coach. Kanyan. It was one of the most powerful houses in the city. They were in good standing with the king. *Or they* were *in good standing with the king,* Hamal thought.

The swordsman snickered, as if the hammer-wielder had told a good joke.

"Don't forget!" Hammer-man insisted. "The House of Kanyan."

They climbed back into the coach and drove away. The driver snapped a whip at the horses, and the coach slid through the snow at a speed that wasn't safe.

Hamal stared after them until the coach rounded a corner.

"I don't think those men were lost," he decided and then looked at the "message" they had left bleeding in the street.

The man wasn't moving. Hamal cocked his head and listened for a heartbeat. The wind was loud and insistent tonight, and so he had to move closer. About four steps away from the man, the familiar sound of a heart finally reached him, but the beat was faint and growing fainter. They had certainly killed this man. He was dying rapidly.

Hamal rubbed his hands together and cupped them to his mouth, blowing hot air into his fingers. He hadn't done this in a while, and most of the wounds he treated now were burns. His friends the flamemakers weren't injured by fire of course, but they could be injured by lightning from the weathermakers. The two elements were different, Hamal supposed, though it seemed a little odd to him why they would be. Both produced heat. Just lightning produced something *more*. And sometimes he thought it seemed very angry.

He pulled up the man's blood-drenched tunic and laid his hand on the wound. The open skin was warm against his fingers, and beneath his touch it began to shift, responding to Hamal's gift. He sealed the vessels back together—that was always the first step, to stop the bleeding—and then he began to repair the tissue. The human body was like fabric; it often needed sewing. There were multiple broken bones and more bruises than he could count, but he wouldn't worry about those—not just now, out in the middle of the street, in the snow. He could fix all of those later.

The blood tried to speak to him, but he ignored it. He was busy. The bones tried to start a conversation, but he ignored them, too.

The initial process didn't take him long. He was usually quick. But as always, he left a scar. He wasn't *that* talented of a healer. Some healers could leave the skin as fresh as an infant's, but even when the cut was small, Hamal had never been able to make the skin perfect. He was good with bones, but skin? There were certain things he couldn't fully heal because of scar tissue.

The man didn't awaken, but that was normal. Brushes with death could leave the mind a little…absent for a while. The body needed time to recover.

Hamal looked the man over. "I need better lighting," he muttered.

There was blood all over the face; he could see that much, despite the shadows of night and snow. The eyes were swollen. The man had been hit repeatedly. The real damage, however—besides the sword through the chest—was the man's right hand. Hamal understood now why that man in the black armor had been carrying a hammer. The hand was just destroyed. Every bone broken—not just cracked, but beaten into shards. Why beat a man's hand this way? Especially if you were just going to kill him later? It seemed rather rude.

Hamal lifted his head and frowned up at the clouds and the falling snow. It was cold. He was cold. Standing to his feet, he stared down at the man and listened to a heartbeat that was stronger now. "Good. You'll be fine, won't you? I'm sorry about the scar."

On the other side of the barrow, there was a mission that took in the weak and injured. They fed them, clothed them, and let them heal. They had good healers working there. Hamal had once seen them heal a man's foot that was turning black and stank with gangrene.

But the mission was next to King's River, the massive body of water that cut the city in half—it was blocks and blocks away from here. It would be better to take this man to the Kladis Tunnel, Hamal decided finally. The tunnel and the warmth offered by the flamemakers were only five or six blocks north of his current position. That was a much easier distance.

But how to get him there? Hamal was not a strong man. He had small hands and small arms, not good for lifting anything, especially not a dead weight like this man was going to be. Richart used to tease him and say, "It's a good thing you're a healer, because you would never make it as anything else." And it was true. After his removal from Richart's house, Hamal had tried to find work, but no one was interested. Most houses in North Barrow already had at least half a dozen healers on their staff—men and women who had been born in the house, so they were at an advantage— and like Richart said, Hamal was too small to do anything else. He had been willing to do anything.

Then the king had died, and no one in North Barrow had wanted to hire anybody new. So Hamal sometimes went and helped at the mission where they were careful with him and never let him have any of the tough cases. It was true that he was a little slow in his thoughts. He knew this. He became confused easily. That was true, too. They were kind to him at the mission, just as the flamemakers were kind, and they gave him only the easy cases— the scrapes and bruises. Never the broken bones. Never anything with lots of blood—of course, most of the blood cases died before they could reach the mission. If you were going to be doing any fighting, it was best to have a healer as a friend.

Hamal crouched down next to the body. "My lord," he said, remembering what the soldier had called this man. "I'm going to drag you. I'm sorry about the snow. I'll work the frostbite from your hands when we get there." He paused. "If you get frostbite."

He crept around to the man's boots and took hold of the cuffs of his trousers, one hand on each pant leg. "Here we go," he called over his shoulder. He stood up as best he could and commenced dragging the man down the street. Soon he didn't feel the cold anymore.

2 The People in the Tunnel

It took Hamal an hour to drag the man to the Kladis Tunnel. He slipped in the snow half a dozen times, and his clothes were wet by the time he arrived at the guard station. That was what the flame-emakers called it, but it was really just a large tree, one of the few trees left in South Barrow. A broken wall stood up near the tree, blocking his view of the guards, but he had come this way before so he knew exactly where they were.

"Who comes?" a voice demanded as he approached.

Hamal, out of breath, heaved the passphrase out of his mouth like a boy tossing a stick that was too big for him. "The gods of fire."

The same voice grumbled through the dark, "That you, Hamal?"

"Aye. And a…a friend, I suppose. I have a man back here."

"What does that mean?"

One shadow broke away from the wall and came to investigate. Hamal thought it was Rizen, and he was proved right as red flames flickered across the guard's fingers and he leaned over the fallen lord to examine the face, holding the flames close to the man's skin. Rizen was not much older than a boy. He was the second-born son of the man who had died after striking the king's soldier on the jaw.

He didn't like to talk about his father, and he hated everyone who could even be remotely blamed for his death—the king, the king's soldiers, and just about everyone from North Barrow.

Hamal dropped the wounded man's legs and put his hands on his own knees, doubling over so he could catch his breath.

Rizen glanced at him. "How long have you been dragging him?"

"Not long," Hamal replied, panting. "I'm just small."

Rizen's partner beside the tree—his outline was beginning to look like Druin's—chuckled under his breath. "You *are* small, Hamal."

Hamal grinned. "But I made it!" The injured man was doing even better now. His heartbeat was stronger. The pain was still present, but he was unconscious anyway, and it would not drive him mad before Hamal finished with him.

"Yes," Druin said agreeably, because he was much more agreeable than Rizen. "We can see you made it."

Druin was the only flamemaker in his family, which meant that he was here alone. Like most gifts, flamemakers descended from other flamemakers. The gift was hereditary, yet Druin's mother was a grower, and people whispered that her husband had been a thiever—a gift that played with the eyes. Thievers were like magicians in that they created illusions. For short periods of time, they could make things appear and disappear.

No one really liked thievers...which was why Druin was a flamemaker. Not even thievers' wives liked them, apparently.

"What are you hoping to do with him?" Druin asked.

"I want to take him inside and fix him," Hamal said.

"You found him—like this, on the ground?" Rizen demanded as he brought his glowing hand down the man's body and looked more closely at the tunic. It was just a bloody mess to Hamal, but Rizen seemed to think something more. "This man has money.

You don't find material like this in South Barrow." His voice hardened. "Where did you say you found him?"

"Back there," Hamal replied, gesturing over his shoulder. "On Narrows Street."

"This is a lot of blood, Hamal."

The words almost sounded like a warning, and Hamal had no idea why. He wasn't doing anything dangerous. He told Rizen and Druin what he had seen. "Two men tossed him out of a coach and stabbed him."

"Where?"

"Through the sternum." Hamal crouched down and gently pulled up the man's tunic, showing them the new scar. "See?"

For a moment, the night was quiet.

"By the gods, Hamal," Druin said. "You healed *that*?"

Replacing the tunic with care, Hamal nodded and stood up. "They threw him out of the coach. They stabbed him. I saw it."

"There aren't many coaches in South Barrow," Rizen said slowly.

Trying to be helpful, Hamal supplied, "It was Lord Kanyan's coach."

The fire in Rizen's hand whisked out. He jerked to his feet in a movement Hamal barely saw in the night shadows. He blinked and found Rizen towering over him.

"What?" Rizen said, intense.

"They said it was Kanyan's coach."

"What did they say *exactly*, Hamal? And none of this babbling you sometimes do. Tell it to me clear and straight."

Was Rizen angry? Why was Rizen angry? Hamal leaned away from him. "They said something about defying the House of Kanyan." He pointed at the man on the ground. "They said that *this* was what would happen to anyone who defied the House of Kanyan."

"Did they say what this man did?"

"No."

"You sure, boy?"

Rizen was only a few years older than Hamal. It was always odd when he called Hamal a boy but didn't use the word for himself. "They didn't say anything about what he did, but they really wanted him to die. And they destroyed his hand. Look."

Again, Hamal crouched on the ground. He dug the man's cold hand out of the snow and showed them. Fire leapt across Rizen's fingers so he could see better, and as the light fell across the man's crumpled hand, Druin made a strangled sound and wavered a bit on his feet, as if he might throw up.

This was the first time Hamal had actually studied the hand in any kind of light, and it was worse than it had looked back on Narrows Street. He could see bones through the skin. It made him think of chops hanging in a butcher's window. Only bad men would do something like this to another man.

The anger vanished from Rizen's voice. As he spoke, he began to sound thoughtful. "The House of Kanyan is a powerful house. They must really hate this fellow."

"They looked like they really hated him," Hamal agreed.

Rizen looked over at Druin, who eventually shrugged and answered a question Hamal hadn't heard. "Up to you. We could try it and see."

Hamal stood up, staring warily at the two of them. *Try what and see?* He often missed what other people were saying. It was as if what they said and what he heard were two different things. What did Rizen and Druin wish to try?

Rizen nodded. He jerked his hand, and the flames choked out. "All right, Hamal. You can keep your pet. Take him inside—Druin will help you. Make him well, but when he's awake, I want to talk to him." Druin murmured something, and Rizen grumbled a curse and corrected, "*We* want to talk to him."

"All right," Hamal said quickly, breathing a sigh of relief. He had never thought they would say no to him. Why would they say no? They weren't evil men. They were flamemakers. His friends. But for a moment there, Rizen had looked very angry, and Hamal still wasn't certain why. This fellow on the ground hadn't killed his father—at least that seemed very unlikely.

Druin was bigger than Hamal. He picked up the body with much more ease than Hamal could have and carried the man over his shoulder into the tunnel, Hamal at his heels.

The Kladis Tunnel began beneath Scarlet Road and ran for two blocks, ending beneath an old building that didn't house anything but rats. The tunnel was wide enough to hold five of the coaches Hamal had seen tonight side by side. It was an actual tunnel, not a large drain under the road. He had been living here off and on for the past two years, and he had never seen it run with water. Tonight, about seventy-five people sought it for shelter. He recognized all the faces. This was most of the flamemaker clan. Some of them were out on patrols. Some were stationed at the other entrance, with the rats, just as Rizen and Druin were stationed at this entrance. The moment he stepped inside, he felt delicious warmth. *Finally.* Other than lanterns hanging along the sloping walls or sitting on the ground, the tunnel was free of fire. The flamemakers didn't need fires, did they? They could *make* fire. Heat rolled off their skin, warming everything around them.

Two men jumped up and came to help Druin with the wounded man. They eased him to the floor next to Cally's lantern and made all sorts of racket when they saw the blood.

"He's fine," Hamal said loudly, because most flamemakers didn't listen until they were forced to. "He's fine. He's just sleeping it off."

Cally was a young woman with two small children. Her

husband had been captured in the last riot and taken across the river. It was doubtful she would ever see him again. No one taken by the king's men ever came back. Cally had sad eyes, but she had always been kind to Hamal, and she was kind still.

Druin returned to his post outside, and Hamal started his work.

"Do you need anything?" Cally asked.

He glanced over at her children, who slept close by.

"We won't wake them," she said gently. She always said that because he was often afraid he would. Children were odd to him. He had healed plenty of scrapes and cuts and broken legs, but it seemed that the younger the children were, the more they would cry, even when Hamal made the pain go away.

"Warm water?" he asked. "He's very dirty. I will need to clean him up."

She nodded and grabbed the metal pail sitting by her first daughter's head. The barrow well was far away, and none of the flamemakers made trips there anymore, not since the snows had started. She would fill the pail with snow, melt it down, fill it again, melt it down, and have a full bucket by the time she returned. An easy task for a flamemaker.

Hamal stripped off the man's tunic and tossed it against the tunnel wall. No one would get any more use out of that thing. Hamal had an extra that had always been a little long on him; it might fit this man.

As he worked, the bones tried to speak to him. Bones were history books, more faithful than any tome found in a king's library, but Hamal ignored them. He had learned his lesson in the past, and he didn't want the man's secrets unless the man wanted to share them himself.

A few of the flamemakers gathered around to watch as he repaired three broken ribs and a broken arm, first by softening the bones until they became pliable and claylike. Then he melded the pieces together like a smithy working with iron. He took his time, being careful. He wanted to be careful with this man. And finally—He turned his attention to the mangled hand. He had never seen a wound like this before. It was possible he would not be able to repair it completely. Skin was the only thing holding the elements in any sort of shape, and it wasn't doing it well, with the bones exposed in various places. As Hamal examined the hand, the man groaned, his head rolling to the side, and the flamemakers started giving Hamal advice.

"He should probably stay asleep for this," Lock said.

"Perhaps if you sealed the skin first, you'd have better luck with the bones," Yurry said.

Mare sniffed and wrinkled up her forehead. "I would clean that first," she said, eyeing the hand doubtfully, "if I were you."

Hamal nodded. "Yes, thank you." And then ignored them. That was part of being a healer—ignoring people. Richart had taught him that ignoring the families of patients was one of the best things you could do when you were working. Be nice to them in the beginning. Be nice to them in the end. But don't let them tell you what to do in the middle.

He reached forward and brushed his thumb across the wounded man's forehead. Instantly, his movements relaxed. The groaning stopped.

"What did you do?" Lock demanded. "Put him back to sleep?"

"Sort of," Hamal replied and began to massage the broken hand with both of his own. When a bone was shattered, sometimes the pieces needed help finding one another again. Realizing that every man and woman in the audience was staring at him, he smiled and said helpfully, "This could take some time."

"Doesn't that hurt him?" Yurry asked.

Mare stared at the hand balefully.

"He's unconscious," Hamal answered. "He won't remember."

"Did you really heal this part?" Mare asked. She reached forward and tapped the scar left by the sword.

"Yes."

"He must have been near death."

"Yes, he was." Very close. Touching it, in fact.

"Do you save many lives, Lord Hamal?"

Hamal frowned at her. They all knew he had once studied with one of the healers who lived in North Barrow, and sometimes they pretended not to remember that Hamal lived in South Barrow now. She didn't call him a lord to be nice to him. She was making fun in her gruff, I-will-teach-you sort of way.

Thinking of his work at the mission, he replied, "No. Not many lives."

"Are you going to be able to fix his hand?" Mare nodded toward it.

"I don't know."

"Hmph," she grunted. She waited a moment and then fired off a new topic. "Is it true about the House of Kanyan? What does this fellow have to do with them? Do you know? What did the soldiers say to you? Why didn't they kill you, too? Have you ever *been* to the Kanyan estate in North Barrow? Folks say it's huge. One of the biggest estates in North Barrow."

Cally returned with the bucket and began to chase her fellow flamemakers away. "Go on—shoo. Let him work in peace."

Grumbling, they left one at a time. In a month, they wouldn't let her tell them what to do, but she had just lost her husband. They felt sorry for her. Hamal felt sorry for her, too. She was a pretty lady, and her husband had not deserved what happened to him.

He repaired the hand as best he could while Cally washed the blood off the man's body with the warm water and a rag. She didn't say anything, thankfully, though Hamal would have listened to her before he listened to anybody else here. These people were his friends, but that did not mean they always were polite and understanding. Sometimes they were just rude and tried to call him *Lord Hamal*. He didn't like that, and it usually meant they were annoyed about something.

Rizen came once to check on his progress. "Well?"

"Still working," Hamal replied and pointed at the man's hand. It was coming together, but the tendons weren't quite right. They had been torn off the bones. *What was left of the bones*, he thought.

"Do we know his name yet?"

"Oh, give it a rest, Rizen," Cally snapped. "He's unconscious. Let him be."

And because she was in mourning, he did as she requested. He stalked back out into the dark.

Most of the people in the tunnel eventually went to sleep. At the distant end, a child cried for a while. Hamal was getting tired, more so than usual. He wasn't used to dragging people through the snow, and he wanted to go to sleep, too. He looked at the man's hand.

"What is it?" Cally asked quietly, sitting beside him.

"Why would they take away a man's hand?" Hamal asked.

She studied him a moment. "It's his sword hand," she answered and gently pointed at the palm. "See the callouses? He's a soldier. If not for the king, then for one of the lords probably. They took his hand so that he could not kill them."

Hamal couldn't stop the gasp that rose up his throat. "They took his occupation."

Cally frowned and nodded. "But only if you can't fix it."

"Cally," he said quietly, sighing. "I can't fix this. I am good with bone. He will have movement—he will be able to *use* the hand. But I don't think he will ever be able to hold a sword again, and I am sorry for it."

"Why? Why are you sorry?"

The man was not much older than Hamal—twenty-five. That was the age of his bones. Hamal was a solid eight years younger than this *boy* lying unconscious on the tunnel floor. "They were so mean to him. It was terrible. They beat him, took his occupation, and then killed him."

Cally put her hand on Hamal's shoulder. "But he didn't die. You saved him." She lowered her voice and began to speak slowly and steadily. "Why does it bother you so much that he won't be able to be a soldier anymore? I thought you didn't like soldiers, Hamal."

"I don't like mean soldiers," he corrected. There was a difference between men who were soldiers and men who were mean soldiers. "But I want to make him well."

"You did make him well. You saved his life."

A twenty-five-year-old without the full use of his hand. That was a sad thing. Hamal looked at the hand one more time, felt the tendons that were out of place and refused to be made well, and then set the hand on the floor.

"How long will he sleep?" Cally asked.

"Some hours," Hamal replied softly. And then Rizen and Druin would want to speak to him, and there wasn't anything Hamal could do about it. "Cally, do you know why Rizen is so interested in this man? Is it because he looks like a soldier?"

A look of sorrow flinched through Cally's eyes. Her voice lowered. "I think they mean to ransom him," she whispered. "If he is an enemy of one of the powerful houses, then he likely is from a powerful house himself. Or at the very least, he works for a powerful house that will probably want him back. It is possible we could get enough coin to feed us for a year."

"Ransom?" Hamal repeated in horror. "But that's...they should not do that! Don't they realize what happened to him tonight? He should go home. He needs to go home."

"Oh, Hamal," she said and touched his face. "You are precious in your thoughts. I like you. I think we need more boys like you. Don't listen to Mare when she says mean things. She's just a child without understanding."

Hamal frowned at her. "She's one of the oldest people in the tunnel. She's nearly fifty."

Cally laughed quietly. "Precisely why it is a shame she's such a child." The light in her eyes faded. "Don't fight Rizen, Hamal. He is dangerous, and he will do what he thinks is best, even if it hurts other people. He could hurt you."

"If he hurts me, I will get better. I am a healer."

Cally watched him a moment. "Just do as I say, Hamal. Trust me. You are a good boy, but Rizen is not a good man. You need to be wary around him."

3 What Happened When He Woke Up

Hamal slept near Cally's lantern that night after dutifully eating the leftover stew she forced upon him. When he was warm, he sometimes forgot to eat. Warmth was more important than food.

When he opened his eyes again, early morning sunlight was pouring in at the distant end of the tunnel. The storm had finally broken. This was the first sunlight Hamal had seen in days.

The soldier with the broken hand was still asleep beside him. Cally had covered the man with a blanket. Without sitting up or touching him, Hamal checked the beat of his heart and the passage of air through his lungs. The man was whole and healthy. Except for the hand. Even the bruising had faded. Perhaps Hamal couldn't fully restore him, but there was no pain anywhere in his body, not even the hand. At least there was that.

The tunnel was beginning to wake up. He smelled the sweet scents of food preparation and baking bread—no one could bake as well as a flamemaker. Hamal knew that some of these people hadn't slept at all last night because the flamemakers were careful. There were always men on duty and going on patrols through the area. It was a rare day when the weathermakers were able to sneak up on them. Yet it did happen from time to time, unfortunately, and then Hamal would spend the day putting hands and legs and faces back together and healing scorch marks. Those were the good days. The bad days were when the soldiers came, called in to stop what they thought was a riot, and then everyone would clear out of the tunnel as fast as possible. The injured would be captured, and sometimes, even the uninjured would be taken, if they weren't fast enough.

Lying on his back, his arms under his head, Hamal listened to the sounds of the children playing. Cally was making breakfast, her attention on the black pot in her hands. None of the flamemakers cooked over open flames; they just held the pot or put a hand to it and heated it that way. Hamal could hear her heartbeat. He could also hear the heartbeat of the sleeping soldier next to him.

But then he heard something else—a third heartbeat. A man stood near Hamal's feet, just beyond his line of sight.

It was Rizen. He hadn't slept and seemed to have no intention to do so. Hamal could see the lack of sleep on his face and hear it in the complaints of his body. About ten other men, Rizen's friends, stood in a group behind him. These were the men who ran the flamemaker clan. There had been others, but they had all been killed or taken by the king's soldiers to be sold on the other side of the river.

Hamal sat up slowly.

Rizen stared at Hamal, his eyes filled with a wild light. He nodded toward the soldier. "Get him up."

Cally didn't look up, but her heartbeat increased. Hamal heard the jump.

Turning toward the soldier, Hamal looked down at him and hoped his gift did not run toward the elements. That was, possibly, the one gift Rizen would kill him for. All others would be forgiven, but a weathermaker *and* a soldier? Here in the tunnel…?

Hamal put a hand on the man's shoulder and then, on a whim,

began to increase certain chemicals in the man's body. A healer could make a person feel things physically by *opening* them inside the person. Richart had called it *flooding*. Hamal wanted the man to be calm. It would not be good to wake a soldier under these conditions, surrounded by angry flamemakers. Internally bracing himself, he shook the shoulder beneath his hand, and the man opened his eyes.

Hamal's breath caught.

And all at once, he knew the man's gift.

The eyes were silver. Not *gray*, as eyes could be from time to time, but silver. As metallic as a sword blade. He was a seer.

The seer gift was rare because it didn't like to follow patterns. It liked to skip generations and land haphazardly among a man's offspring. This fellow was a soldier…and a seer. He must have been very good at his job. Seers could perceive the future and the thoughts of a man's heart, and whether he was good or bad, and what he intended. That would make a soldier very valuable.

Hamal stared at him and wondered a great many things— namely, why did the House of Kanyan wish him dead?

The man blinked once. His silver eyes immediately focused on Hamal, who could feel his gaze the way he would feel fingers pushing on his face. He had never met a seer before, but he'd heard that their gaze *felt* different. It actually felt like *something*, and now, having met one, he agreed.

Seers tended to do very well for themselves. He had never heard of a seer living in poverty. There were only a few people with this gift here in the city, and all of them were in the employ of wealthy men or the king himself.

Hamal felt the tension lurch in the soldier's body, and he squeezed the man's shoulder. "Peace," he said. "You're alive. This is the Kladis Tunnel in South Barrow. These are flamemakers. My name is Hamal."

The man blinked again. The concern bled from his system slowly. "You are a healer."

Hamal nodded eagerly. "Yes. How do you know? Can you see it in me?" He didn't know how a seer worked, but it would be interesting to find out.

A gruff scrape of laughter came up the man's throat. He sat up slowly and seemed surprised when he felt no pain. His gaze quickly found Rizen and his group, and he studied them without comment. Hamal had withdrawn his hand, and so he no longer felt the emotions in the man's body. He couldn't *sense* emotions as the feelers did, but because he was a healer, he could sense what passed through flesh. If the emotion was strong enough to be felt physically, and he was touching the man as it occurred, he would be able to sense it.

"Who are you?" Rizen demanded. Hamal noticed that Rizen's hand was on the head of his ax slung through his belt. Most flamemakers preferred axes to swords, though many of the men in this tunnel, and the women, too, used bows.

The soldier stared at Rizen for a long moment without answering. When he finally did answer, he said simply, "Cale Lehman."

"From which house?"

Cale shook his head. "My blood is not of any house. I was not born into a house of standing."

Rizen's eyes narrowed. "Who do you work for?"

The soldier sighed deeply. "No one. Not anymore."

Hamal didn't have to touch him to know what he was feeling. Hamal knew what it was like to lose a master you cared for, a master who was also a friend, and he thought it was the same sort of sadness now in Cale.

"You're lying."

Hamal's head jerked around at Rizen's tone. He stared at the flamemaker in surprise.

Cale's voice hardened. "I do not lie. As a seer, I choose not to lie, for I can see the outcome of every lie I would be tempted to speak. I tell you the truth. My name is Cale Lehman. I do not hail from one of the House Lords. I do not work for one of the House Lords."

Rizen's jaw tightened, but he did not argue. "Why does Kanyan wish you dead?"

Cale stared at him. He blinked once. "I do not know," he replied.

Rizen snorted. "You're a seer. How could you not know?"

"If I could see everything, I would not be here, would I?"

Oh, Hamal thought, pleased. *The seer is clever. He is cleverer than Rizen.*

"I am not without resources," Rizen growled. "I will get the information I seek, whether or not you help me."

Cale nodded. "Please do get it, and then you can tell me why Kanyan wishes to kill me. I would very much like to know this myself."

Rizen snarled something unintelligible, and he did it again when Cale chose to ignore him. The seer looked instead at Hamal, who was sitting there quietly and listening. Again, he could feel the man's gaze. Fingers of sight.

"I remember dying," the seer said quietly.

Hamal nodded. "They killed you. But it was not to death."

The man's brows drew together. "I remember dying," he repeated.

Hamal thought it must be that the seer didn't understand, so he tried gently to explain what had happened: "They beat you badly and put a sword through your chest. Then they left you in the snow. But I saw them leave—I was there. You still had a heartbeat when they left." He shrugged and repeated, "They killed you, but it was not to death."

Perhaps it would be good if he waited to tell him about

his hand. He didn't want Rizen to know. Rizen wouldn't care, and this was something important. Cale had lost his sword hand—such a loss deserved respect.

Cale grunted once in reply. That was all he did.

Rizen snapped, "Don't try to leave," but when that threat was ignored as well, the flamemaker stomped off in a fury. His friends started to go with him, but Rizen commanded a few to stay behind. "To watch him," he said. He made Cale sound like a prisoner, and Hamal didn't understand why. Cale wasn't anybody. He said so. Why hold him prisoner?

Three men—Cot, Mephren, and Sal—sat down at Noble's lantern some distance away and did as Rizen ordered. Hamal thought it strange that he could feel their eyes, yet the sensation was radically different than what he felt whenever Cale looked at him.

Cale looked at him now. "What is it you're not telling me?" he asked quietly.

Hamal twitched in surprise. Lowering his voice, he whispered, "I repaired your body, as much as I could. But I am truly sorry to tell you that I could not repair your sword hand. I did my best, but..." He shook his head, the sadness building in his chest. What news to tell a soldier! "Your enemies destroyed it. You will have some movement, but not enough to hold a sword in combat."

The silver eyes closed and opened in a slow blink. Cale looked down at his hands in his lap and tested them. The left made a strong fist; the right closed, but loosely. He could not get the ends of his fingers to press hard against the heel of his hand.

A quiet moment passed around Cally's lantern. She tended to breakfast, glancing at Cale from time to time, and Hamal could hear the voices of laughing children and serious adults echoing through the tunnel. But at Cally's lantern, all was quiet.

Cale took a deep breath and said at last, "You have given me back my life. I can survive without a hand." He lifted his head, and the silver eyes glinted intently as he studied Hamal. "Why are you here?"

Hamal shrugged. "The flamemakers are my friends. I enjoy their warmth."

Cale looked at Cally, who met his gaze, though she seemed not to like it. Hamal thought for a moment that she would pull back and look away. Cale's gaze was something you could feel. It was odd, but not in a bad way.

"Hamal is a good boy," she told him fiercely and frowned at Cale as Hamal blushed. He wished she wouldn't say things like that to strangers.

Another moment of quiet came and went.

"Yes," Cale said. "I can see that he is a good boy." And then quite unexpectedly, he added, "When the time comes, he will tell seers what to do."

Hamal again felt surprise. He was just a healer, and not even a great one. A good one perhaps. But not great. He had not been able to give the man back his hand.

The silver eyes swung toward him. "Why are you here?" Cale asked a second time.

As he often did, Hamal began to wonder what he was missing. The question sounded short to him—predictable. Something he could understand. But apparently, he did not understand the question at all. "This is where I live. With the flamemakers."

"Why do you live in South Barrow?"

"Because I don't live anywhere else," Hamal answered.

Cale fell silent, but he watched Hamal steadily, and after a while, his stare began to make Hamal laugh on the inside. He wasn't interesting. He was just a healer—a boy with a small form and a brain that was a little slow. He wasn't interesting.

Cally put a bowl of porridge in his hands and made him eat. She liked to feed him. Did she think he was starving to death?

She certainly acted like it.

Cally fed the seer as well. "You are welcome at my lantern," she told him curtly, adding, "For as long as Rizen allows it."

Cale dipped his head once and politely thanked her for the food.

4 The Poor Horse

Usually after breakfast, Hamal went across the barrow to the mission beside the river and helped the healers who worked there. The weather was good today, and it would have been a pleasant walk through town, but instead, he decided he was going to stay in the tunnel with Cale. It wasn't Cally's job to look after the poor man Hamal had dragged home last night; it was Hamal's job, the first job he'd had in two years. He liked Cale, and he decided that he would be friends with him. He had never had a seer as a friend. It might prove interesting.

As he sat down next to Cale against the tunnel wall, the seer turned and looked at him.

"What are you doing?" Cale asked.

"I'm sitting down," Hamal replied.

"Yes, I can see that. Why are you sitting?"

Hamal gave him a warm smile. "Because I thought I would keep you company." Straightening his legs out in front of him, he heaved a contented sigh and then waved his hand toward the activity happening all around them. "Bunch of flamemakers. They don't really like anyone but other flamemakers." He paused. "I'm sorry, by the way."

Cale's silver gaze was always intense. "Why?"

"I brought you here last night so you would be warm and so I could finish healing you. I didn't know what Rizen was going to do."

His voice low, Cale asked, "What is he going to do?"

Hamal grunted. The idea was ridiculous. He had thought Rizen smarter than this. All the flamemakers said that Rizen was smart. "They all think you're someone, when you told them you were no one. They think your house that doesn't exist will give them money."

"A ransom," Cale said quietly. His gaze never wavered from Hamal's face, but for a moment it grew extremely focused, as if he could see something written on the back of Hamal's head.

Hamal nodded and then said again, "I'm sorry, but I couldn't have taken you anywhere else. It was snowing hard. You were unconscious."

"What did you mean when you said you brought me here to finish the healing?"

Hamal knew this man was smart—smarter than Rizen, so the question made him feel like he was missing something. Again. He had told Cale all these things before. "That man killed you, Cale. He put his sword through your chest. You were bleeding. Your heart was giving out. So obviously, I had to fix that wound first, or you would have died."

"So you healed the sword wound. Right there in the street."

"You would not have lasted to have it fixed anywhere else. I told you."

For the first time since Hamal sat down, Cale turned his head away and looked through the tunnel. He didn't seem overly interested in anything that was going on around him, yet still he looked. "Was it difficult for you?"

"It was difficult to drag you for six blocks." Hamal laughed. Small hands.

Cale's silver eyes came upon him again. "Was it difficult for you to heal a wound as severe as mine?"

Hamal shrugged. "That part was not difficult. Your hand was difficult."

For several minutes, Cale was quiet and returned to watching the flamemakers move through the tunnel. Many of the parents had small jobs here and there in the barrow, so at this hour—about mid-morning—the tunnel held children mostly. Once a week, a tutor came from West Barrow and taught the children their letters and numbers. It was kind of him, Hamal thought, a good sort of charity, but half the adults who lived in this tunnel could read even less than their children could. It would be nice if West Barrow sent a tutor for the adults as well, but Hamal didn't know if the adults would accept tutoring at this point in their lives. Flamemakers could be a peculiar, proud group of people. Hamal could read and write, thanks to his father's diligence long ago, but he wasn't good with numbers. They were like a foreign language to him.

The men Rizen had left still watched from Noble's lantern. Noble had one eye and a limp from a fight with a weathermaker fifteen years ago. He never left the tunnel now unless they came under attack. He was several years older than Mare—a very old man by the harsh standards of South Barrow.

Cale asked, "Do you often heal mortal wounds?"

Hamal shook his head. He liked that Cale was willing to talk to him. Flamemakers didn't always like to talk, which was one reason he usually trotted over to the mission every day. "Not anymore."

His tone steeped with patience, Cale asked, "When did you heal mortal wounds on a regular basis?"

"Two years ago," Hamal replied. "I used to live in North Barrow in the House of Sangren." To be helpful he said, "It is located by the tributary not far from the king's palace." But maybe Cale already knew that. The House of Sangren was one of the powerful houses.

Cale's head turned, the motion slow. As the fellow looked at him, Hamal began to wonder if Cale knew how to move quickly. Maybe that was how he had been captured by the evil men—he moved too slowly.

"Richart Sangren was a good man," Hamal said. "We worked together. He was a healer, like I am. He taught me many things, and we experimented with different types of healings on different animals. Horses mostly. Well, just one horse over and over again. That poor fellow had his legs broken half a dozen times. He lost both ears. We poisoned him a few times...I know it sounds awful, and I felt bad for it, but Richart insisted we practice. He was the one who did the cutting. I don't like injuring things."

The seer blinked once. "And you were the one who did the repairs?" he asked quietly.

"Aye."

Cale considered Hamal a moment. His silver gaze prodded Hamal's face. "Why were you dismissed from the House of Sangren?"

Hamal never had the opportunity to talk like this, so he would gladly take it. He would tell the man anything he wanted to know. "Richart died. His son became the new lord of the house, and he didn't know what Richart and I used to practice together. Richart kept it secret. He wrote books about healing, and he called what we were doing *research*." Hamal thought about it and rubbed absently at a stain on his trousers. "I think I was dismissed because the son didn't like Richart, his father. They argued all the time—shouted with full voices. When Richart was murdered, I couldn't heal him so I was sent away."

Several moments passed. Cale watched him for the duration. "How did Richart die?" he asked.

"Same way you did," Hamal replied. "He was attacked."

Another slow blink. "How is it that you did not save him?"

A familiar twinge flickered through Hamal's chest. He was a good healer, but he was not a *great* healer. He left scars, and sometimes he couldn't save his friends. "He wasn't found for a full day. He didn't come to his office—no one knew where he was, and by the time his body was found, his soul was gone. There is nothing I can do for a dead man who has been dead for that length of time. His son told me to try, and I did try, but I couldn't save him."

Cale looked through the tunnel. His silver gaze hovered around Noble's lantern for a time before passing on. He appeared calm, but there was something strange about his movements. It was like he thought the flamemakers were trying to listen to their conversation. Hamal scratched the top of his head and tried to figure out why Cale would think they—he and Cale—were telling secrets. This wasn't secret information, and even if it were, these were his friends—even Rizen. Perhaps they were a little dangerous, but Cale wasn't actually worried about danger. Hamal could hear the steady beat of his heart; there was no fear in it.

"How many times have you repaired a wound as severe as mine?" Cale asked.

Hamal leaned his head back against the tunnel wall and thought about it. A wound like Cale's? Wounds were all different—as unique as people's stories. None of them were the same, so the question was a little confusing. Hamal had healed severe wounds before, but none of them had involved exactly what Cale's had involved. For instance, most of the time there hadn't been any snow.

He decided that maybe Cale meant severe wounds that had happened recently. Hamal had to count on his fingers and ended up on the third finger of his right hand, after starting on his left. "Eight," he said. He laughed quietly. "But five times, it was the horse. That poor fellow."

"Am I number eight?"

"I think so."

Cale closed his eyes, opened them. "You do not remember?"

"I've never been good with numbers."

LAUREN STINTON

When Cale asked, Hamal told him about the other men he had saved. South Barrow was the most dangerous district in the city. Poverty drove men to extreme actions, and it wasn't safe to walk the streets alone, not at night, and sometimes not even during the day. Even now, guards were posted up and down the tunnel and outside both entrances. Everyone was cautious in South Barrow. Everyone was afraid. Hamal felt comfortable moving about in the nighttime only because he was a healer. If he were a grower or a feeler—especially if he were a feeler—he would never travel by himself after dark.

The first man had been attacked by thieves in an alley. Hamal had come upon the body in time to hear the thieves still running up the street. The man's throat was cut, and Hamal had healed him and then dragged his body into an empty storage box in the alley. It had been a warm night in the fullness of summer; the injured man could sleep outside without worry of the cold. Hamal stayed with him, and then in the morning when the man awakened, they chatted a few minutes—Hamal did enjoy conversation—and then the man left. His wife was waiting for him, he said.

The second man had been gutted in the middle of Poorman's Market. Hamal had scooped his entrails back into him, and that man had not actually lost consciousness at any point in the process. He had walked away afterward on his own power.

The third man had been knifed under the Ghost Bridge, near the West Barrow wall.

The fourth man had come looking for Hamal, carrying his own hand. Someone he had barely seen had attacked him in the dark and chopped it off. He had lost a lot of blood by the time he staggered into Hamal's presence.

When Hamal was finished with his tales, Cale nodded slowly. "You are right."

"About what?" Hamal asked.

"You are bad with numbers. What happened with the man who lost his hand?"

Hamal shrugged. "I put it back on. It isn't hard, you know? It's healing, the same as anything else. It just needs to be done quickly, before the limb dies. He still has a scar—nasty thing. But his hand works."

Again, Cale scanned the children and the adults in the tunnel. His voice lowered. "Did you try to find work as a healer after the House of Sangren dismissed you?"

"Aye. There was nothing to be had."

"I suppose people thought you weren't very good at healing."

Would this man ever stop surprising him? Hamal laughed once and said, "How did you know? That's what they said at every house I tried. They said I wasn't very good." He shrugged again. It didn't matter what they thought. He had come to terms with it. He was a good healer, just not great.

"Richart kept you a secret." Cale's metallic eyes narrowed as he studied Hamal. "That's why he had you work on the horse and not a human patient. It is widely known through the Three Barrows that Richart Sangren was the most talented healer since the Barrow Wars. The king had been pressuring him to be his personal healer. What do you think of that?" He watched Hamal carefully.

The Three Barrows was an alliance between the three districts that gave back to society, instead of existing on charity. What could South Barrow offer the others? They had nothing but riots between the weathermakers and the flamemakers—and poverty. They had plenty of poverty. "He was a good friend," Hamal replied.

"Do you think he was a talented healer?"

"Oh, yes. He was very good."

"Why didn't he heal himself when he was stabbed?"

Hamal cringed. The memory still kept him awake at night if he thought about it for too long. "They cut off his hands. He couldn't touch the wounds to heal them, because he had no hands. If you want to kill a healer, that's what you do. You take his way to heal himself."

Cale nodded slowly. He stared at Hamal a moment or two more and then returned his attention to the passing flamemakers. Flamemakers did not like to sit still. Hamal might not be very bright, but these people moved so frequently that even he had noticed. They were like the fire they contained—one whiff of a breeze and off they went. Cally had gone to work—she helped at a small bakery on North Street—and Hamal could see her two little girls playing with other children down the tunnel.

After a long time, Cale said, "Thank you for saving my life, Hamal."

Hamal grinned. "You picked a convenient location for your death. Dying in plain sight on the street helped me a great deal."

A smile turned the seer's mouth. It was a first smile. Hamal had not seen him express any sign of pleasure or happiness before this. "You're welcome. Should I choose to die again in the future, I hope you are somewhere nearby."

5 The King's Men

Hamal sat with Cale for most of the day. From time to time, the two of them got up and walked because Hamal knew that Cale was a soldier, or had been a soldier, and he imagined that soldiers needed movement. They would walk the length of the tunnel twice and then return to the wall to sit next to Cally's lantern.

Hamal thoroughly enjoyed Cale's company, so much so that he forgot Cale was a prisoner. Rizen's three men got up and followed every time Hamal and Cale started off down the tunnel, but the flamemakers hung back a ways, not close enough to hear Hamal's conversation with Cale. Whenever Hamal did remember them, he knew the distance had nothing to do with giving them privacy. More likely, they just didn't want to hear the conversation. None of those three men seemed to like conversation very much. Every time Hamal tried to speak with them, they made excuses and moved away. Cale, however, asked questions and answered them and never gave a single excuse about anything.

At the beginning of their third walk, Cale suddenly halted and looked south, toward the entrance of the tunnel beneath Scarlet Road. His silver eyes seemed to spark as the distant light caught them.

"What is it?" Hamal asked.

Cale nodded toward the tunnel entrance. "Soldiers are headed this way. The king's men."

"Soldiers?" Hamal felt his heartbeat quicken. He turned and followed Cale's gaze, but all he saw was the tunnel's circular ceiling and the flamemakers moving about. Soldiers in the Kladis Tunnel meant trouble. It meant more sales on the other side of the river.

"Yes. A division of sixty." To Hamal, it seemed that Cale could see the soldiers with his naked eyes, as if the tunnel had disappeared all around him. "Masly is with them."

"Who is Masly?" Hamal asked.

"Another seer," Cale replied. He paused and added quietly, "He works closely with the king."

That didn't sound like business as usual. As far as Hamal knew, the soldiers who came to put down the riots had never been accompanied by a seer. Cale was the first seer Hamal had met—or even seen from a distance. "Why would a seer who works for the king come here with soldiers?"

Cale blinked once and looked at him.

Hamal shifted self-consciously, sensing it had been a foolish question, though he couldn't see why. He reached up and rubbed his head. "What?"

Cale did not make fun of him. They had talked all day today, and not once had Cale made him feel silly. "He's likely looking for a body," Cale said softly.

"Whose body?"

Cale smiled slightly, but even then, it was in fun, not in *making* fun. He was different than a flamemaker, more gentle. "My body. He likely can see that I was brought here, and they expect to collect a corpse."

"We need to tell Rizen," Hamal said. He tried to sound as calm as Cale did, but it was difficult. Soldiers meant trouble. They never came to the tunnel unless they wanted something—like flame-makers to sell on the other side of the river.

"They're already at the flamemakers' checkpoint," Cale said. "Rizen knows they are here."

Sounds of commotion began to drift from the tunnel entrance. It didn't sound like an attack or a fight, more like arguments, but Hamal still had to force his concern away. He wasn't worried about himself—if he ever got arrested, he could just heal people in the prison. It would be the healthiest prison in King's Barrow! Or if they sold him across the river, then he would just keep on heal-ing flamemakers. Maybe weathermakers, too, if they let him. Not much would change.

But he was worried for his friends. The flamemakers had lost so many members already, and it seemed unlikely that the king's men had come for only one body—and a dead one at that.

Cale set his hand on Hamal's shoulder. Hamal twitched once in surprise, looking up at him, and realized suddenly that very few people had touched him in South Barrow. Why was that?

"Hamal," Cale said softly, "not all of these men who are coming to the tunnel are good men. Just as I can see that you are faithful, I can see that some of them are unfaithful. I don't know which ones, and I couldn't tell you what is amiss with them…but I can tell you it would be wise to avoid them."

Startled, Hamal began to pull away, but Cale's fingers dug into his shoulder. "You lived in North Barrow for ten years. Were you never exposed to politics in all that time?"

Hamal didn't understand the question and finally sputtered, "I…I don't think so. Richart kept me at his side most of the time, and whenever he left the office, I stayed behind with his books."

The silver eyes prodded him. "For ten years, you never inter-acted with any nobleman other than Richart?"

Hamal shrugged. "Why would I? I worked with Richart."

"Hmm." Cale nodded as he studied him, the movement slow and thoughtful. He moved his hand away. "What do you know about the king's death?"

Hamal sucked in a breath. "What?" he whispered, his stomach in his throat.

"King Landan," Cale supplied quickly. "Cedrick's father. Two years ago, a short time after Richart's death, King Landan died of a stroke before his healers could reach him."

Hamal calmed. "Yes," he said. Hearing the tension in his own voice, he took a deep breath and tried again: "Yes, I heard about that. I was still in North Barrow at the time—it was a very sad business. He was a good king." The entire city had mourned his death. His son Cedrick perhaps would be a good king as well, but Hamal thought it was difficult to tell about a king when that king had only two years of practice.

"Well, some people disagree with that assessment, Hamal. And some people disagree about the son as well. Not everyone is as loyal to the throne as you are." Cale paused, staring with his silver eyes toward the distant mouth of the tunnel. As the tunnel erupted with sudden cries of fear and outrage, he said, sounding surprised, "Oh. They arrested Rizen."

Sudden mayhem hit the tunnel like floodwaters. Everyone knew what it meant to be arrested by the king's soldiers. Your goodbyes would never be said. Your face would never be seen again. A familiar sort of fear dropped across Hamal's shoulders as the flamemakers started running for the secondary exit beneath the warehouse.

He didn't think. He just acted. "Quick," he urged Cale, grabbing the man's arm. "We have to go."

Cale didn't say a word. He followed Hamal—and dozens and dozens of others—up the tunnel and into the warehouse, where the flamemakers scattered. They all knew what to do. They had done this before. Half an hour later, Hamal found himself with Cale, alone, near the mission. He had no idea when Rizen's guards—the three watchmen—had stopped following them. He had lost sight of them in the warehouse. Perhaps, with Rizen taken, they didn't care about Cale anymore. Rizen was the brains behind the plan to ransom the man—and they all knew what would happen to Rizen now.

"I'm sorry," Hamal said, breathing hard as he leaned against the brick wall of an abandoned creamery.

Cale glanced at him. "For what?"

"You know those people. I didn't think about that—that you know them. They are your friends. They could take you back to North Barrow. If you wish, we could go back, and you could meet up with them."

Cale shook his head. "They were looking for a body. I told you."

Hamal looked at him sharply.

A soft smile turned the corner of Cale's mouth. "Mine. My body, Hamal. They expect to find me dead. Why is that, do you think?"

Hamal thought about it, and the answer slowly became obvious. "Because they know about Kanyan's coach. They know those bad men killed you."

"How do you think they know?"

Hamal swallowed. "Someone told them."

"Exactly. I do not want to go back to North Barrow with those men, Hamal. I think…" Cale hesitated. "They came to find a body, not a man alive. I think that if I returned with them, a body is what they would present before the king. A body as dead as the one they expected to find. If you will come with me, Hamal, I know of a safe place we could go."

Hamal didn't know what this man knew and what he didn't. Cale was a mystery. They had talked for most of the day, but Hamal was the one who had used the words, because he got to use them so rarely. Cale had mostly listened and asked questions. So right now, Hamal knew very little of the man. He had not talked about his history whatsoever. What safe place did Cale know of in South Barrow?

"All right," Hamal replied. With the soldiers in control of the tunnel, he had nowhere else to go except the mission, and he really didn't want to go there. Not anymore. They wouldn't let him stay the night anyway.

Cale did not take him to a safe place in South Barrow. Three hours later, they were standing in the central court of a large house in North Barrow, across the river. Years had passed since Hamal had seen a house this expansive. The walls surrounding the central court were at least thirty feet high, and every corner Hamal saw—every edge and every point—was coated in gold.

"Where are we?" he whispered to Cale as the heavily armed guards along the walls frowned at him. They ignored Cale, but Hamal they watched like hawks watching a mouse. Cale sent a servant for the master of the house, and Hamal shivered as they waited, though it had nothing to do with the cold. The vast court, with all its statues and flowing fountains—running water even in the winter!—was warm somehow, as if every man guarding the walls was a flamemaker.

"This is the House of Kanyan," Cale answered, and that was when Hamal realized he had made friends with a crazy man.

6 The House of Kanyan

"But the House of Kanyan killed you!" Hamal protested—quietly, so the guards along the walls wouldn't hear.

Cale calmly shook his head. "No, they didn't."

Hamal seized Cale's arm. "But they *did* kill you. I saw them do it!"

He looked wildly through the court—and realized slowly that the soldiers in this court wore silver armor with a red-and-gold sparrow on the right shoulder, crafted in such a way that it looked like it was made of fire. They did not wear black armor, like the men who had injured Cale, but did that matter? Maybe they had just been *disguised* that night in South Barrow, so the king's soldiers at the bridge wouldn't recognize them.

Cale smiled at Hamal warmly. Indeed, the warmth in the smile took Hamal aback. They were talking about serious things! And Cale was unconcerned! "You are a good person, Hamal. I appreciate your thoughts and the way in which you think them. If you wanted someone to believe something, how would you go about making him believe you?"

Hamal didn't understand. "I would tell him."

Cale nodded. "Yes, you would. You would tell him. But what if you wanted him to believe something that wasn't true? What if you wanted to spread a *rumor* instead of the truth? Those men you saw did not work for Kanyan. They are members of an uprising against the king. They *told* you they worked for Kanyan because they were trying to throw suspicion on his house and make him sound like a traitor. They lied."

Hamal rubbed the top of his head as he listened. "Cale," he said at last. "I believe you are much smarter than I."

Cale laughed. "But when I look at you, Hamal, I see that is not true. What do you make of that?"

Hamal heard a door bang on the distant side of the court, and two finely dressed men—they had to be lords of the house—ran out to meet Cale. Hamal stared in surprise because he had never seen a lord run anywhere. He wasn't sure what surprised him more—that they were running at all or that they ran the same way poor men did.

The older man grabbed Cale by flinging both arms about him. The second man looked very much like the first, but a younger version, closer to Cale's age. Hamal suspected that if he touched them, he would surely learn that they were father and son. The bones would tell you a man's age and history. The blood would tell you his family line—the blood he came from and how many sons and daughters he had produced. The son wore a huge smile and seemed as happy to see Cale as his father was.

"Good to see you, Cale Lehman," said the first, finally letting Cale go. "Good to see you. Wild rumors run amok through the barrow, and most of them say you are dead. I am glad to see it isn't true."

Cale bowed his head, showing deference to the man who clearly loved him, and said quietly, "May we speak in private, my lord?"

The smile vanished from the lord's face. "Yes. Yes, of course."

Hamal had felt invisible for the first part of the meeting, but when the lord abruptly looked at him, he remembered what you were supposed to do around lords and went to bow, only to have Cale's hand snap around his arm, keeping him upright.

"This way," Cale said and urged him sideways. Hamal stumbled the first few steps as Cale herded him through the courtyard and then through a tall doorway into the house.

The hall beyond the door was well lit and red. Everything was red—the marble, the carpets, the lamps. The second hallway they entered was also red but had some yellow, too, and the hallway after that was just yellow. Hamal thought it was somewhat like walking through a very large but muted bonfire. The colors weren't overwhelming, just everywhere.

Cale stopped in front of a doorway guarded by two men wearing the sparrow-shouldered armor. One of them quickly opened the door for him, and Hamal found himself pulled into a dark office. A single lamp blazed at each end of the room, and the air was warm in here, just as it had been in the hallways. There were no windows, and the walls were lined with more books than Hamal had seen in his life. Not even Richart had owned this many books. He wondered if the lord had written any of these, because most of the books Richart had were ones he had written himself. Perhaps that was how it was done in North Barrow—lords and ladies wrote their own books.

Cale released Hamal's arm, and as soon as the door was closed, he said quietly, looking Hamal in the eyes, "Forgive me. I just don't want anyone to know who you are. Or at least, I want them to be very confused about who you are. My lords, this is Hamal. He is a healer I met in South Barrow."

The older lord grunted. "So the rumors of your death are not entirely untrue, I take it."

Cale smiled calmly. Hamal could hear elevated heartbeats in

both lords, but the beat of Cale's heart was calm, almost serene. "Hamal, these are the first and second lords of Kanyan—Mercen and his son Rhyan." He paused. "They are both as loyal to the throne as you are. You may take my word for it. They, along with most of their staff, are flamemakers, which I trust will help you feel at home among them. If you are willing, I would like you to tell the story of the night you found me."

Hamal looked from Mercen and Rhyan to Cale and frowned, asking tentatively, "You are certain of this?" The story made the Kanyans look like traitors.

"Yes. Go ahead."

So Hamal told the story. He was not a very good storyteller, though he loved the process; he tended to repeat himself and emphasize points no one else thought very important, when they seemed very important to him. He talked about the man with the hammer and the man with the sword and what they had said about the House of Kanyan. They had slain Cale in the street, and Hamal frowned a lot—he could feel it—as he explained how he had been unable to save Cale's hand. The tendons were destroyed. He had pieced them back together but barely, and he was sorry that he had been unable to do a better job. He was a good healer, not a great one. He always left scars.

Cale was standing there with his arms folded, watching the lords of Kanyan. No one interrupted Hamal during the telling, which Hamal found gratifying, for he was always interrupted when he tried to tell stories in the Kladis Tunnel.

When he had finished, the lords of Kanyan stared at him.

Eventually, Mercen snorted. "Is that all?"

Hamal pulled back in surprise and glanced at Cale, who smiled at him reassuringly. "This is his way of conveying that he is impressed," the seer said.

Mercen muttered half a dozen things that, to Hamal, didn't sound very impressed.

"What were you doing in that coach, Cale?" Rhyan asked. He had a deeper voice than Hamal expected. He sounded like an orator Hamal had heard calling from a stage in the North Barrow market.

Cale gave no outward sign of tension or anger, but his heart jumped. Hearing the leap, Hamal looked at him in concern.

"Whose men met you in my coach?" Mercen demanded. "And it was my coach. It was stolen right out of the west stable two nights ago, and the city patrol found it last night near the Burberry Bridge." A moment passed in tense quiet. "Was that your blood inside it?"

As calm as ever, Cale ignored the question and replied, "They were Masly's men."

Hamal looked at Cale in surprise. The seer in the tunnel? Cale had said nothing about this.

Mercen's dark eyes narrowed. "You have seen this? You are certain?"

"I cannot tell you that they were Masly's men directly, but I can tell you that they are associated with him in some way. They claim an allegiance with him. However, I do not have proof of this, and as you know, a seer's word is not enough in any court. There must be proof."

Mercen cursed loudly. He was a flamemaker all right. "So you thought it would be wise to go jump in a coach with those men and—what? Just see what would happen? Masly is the most talented seer in an age. I know you're upset about the prince's death, Cale, but by the gods—"

"What did you see?" Rhyan interrupted. Hamal liked him better than he did the first lord. He seemed more polite. "Did you see something that made you get into that coach? You're not a fool,

Cale, no matter what my father suggests."

Mercen snorted a second time. He had been so relieved to see Cale alive, but all that seemed to be forgotten now. He just looked upset. Hamal did not understand lords.

"You must have known it was a trap," Rhyan insisted. "Yet you got into the coach anyway. What did you see that was so important that you threw your life to the wind to try and obtain it?"

Cale drew a breath. Hamal listened as the beat of his heart grew quiet again. Rhyan and Mercen both leaned forward to hear his words.

"I saw," Cale said after a momentary stillness, "that by accepting what was clearly a trap, I would save the kingdom through the hand of a humble man. That man would be waiting for me where the coach stopped."

Rhyan's eyes widened. So did Mercen's. They began to look a little like fish gasping on the bottom of a boat. They stared at Cale. Then all three men turned and stared at Hamal.

Hamal couldn't help himself. His head went back, and he laughed until his face hurt. "You, sir," he sputtered, pointing at Cale, "are the bravest man I have ever met."

Cale grinned, looking pleased. "Thank you, Hamal."

"You think I'm going to help you save something? How am I supposed to do that? I don't know much about kings—I don't even know much about lords."

"But you do know about healing." Cale tilted his head to the side and asked, "Have you ever wondered why there aren't many healers in South Barrow?"

Hamal shrugged. "We have healers. There are plenty of healers at the mission. Good healers, too. I once saw them heal a foot that was black and smelled of gangrene."

"What makes a man a good healer?"

"If he does his job well and takes care of people."

Cale's head tilted a little more. "Was Richart Sangren a good healer?"

He had already asked this question. Why was he asking it again? "Yes," Hamal replied cautiously. There must be a reason Cale was asking—again.

Mercen took a step forward and said intently, "Hamal, you knew Richart Sangren?"

"He studied with him for ten years," Cale replied. He turned to Hamal abruptly. "Isn't that right, Hamal? Isn't that what you told me? You said that Richart did the cutting, and you did the healing. Isn't that...right? Richart called it research."

Hamal looked at Cale with suspicion. "Yes."

Mercen suddenly looked less like a flamemaker and more like a feeler. His face paled. His heartbeat seemed to halt for a breath and then doubled its pace. "You were...you were Richart's healer?"

"I worked with him. I never *healed* him." Hamal added a moment later, "My lord." He had been away from lords for two years. He was forgetting his manners. As he realized what he had just said, his stomach swam. *I never healed Richart, though I tried.*

"Richart Sangren was butchered. They cut off his hands, and he died from multiple stab wounds to the chest. You healed Cale here—why didn't you heal Richart, if you *worked* with him?"

Hamal could hear the sarcasm in the first lord's voice and those words stung in ways nothing else could, but he didn't try to make him understand. He was here with Cale, because Cale was his friend. Lord Mercen was not his friend, and Hamal knew how stubborn flamemakers could be. "He was killed in secret. No one found the body for hours and hours. He was dead by the time I saw him. I can't do anything for a dead man who's been dead—he's dead. My lord."

Cale looked closely at Hamal, studying him as if he were a book. His silver gaze grew intense, and then he reached down and grabbed Hamal's hand, setting it on his chest—on Cale's chest. Mercen and Rhyan both pulled back and seemed surprised. But Cale was happy. Hamal was immediately aware of this, with his hand on Cale's chest. Cale's heartbeat was strong and healthy, and his entire body filled with the physical signatures of contentment and happiness.

"Why are you so happy?" Hamal asked.

Cale grinned. "I'm just glad you're here. I'm going to ask you the same question I did before."

"You do that a lot."

The grin widened. "Yes. I know." Keeping Hamal's hand pinned to his chest, Cale asked again, "Have you ever wondered why there aren't many healers in South Barrow? I know there are healers who work at the mission—but there are no healer *clans*. Families of healers don't live together in the barrow the way the flamemakers do. Why is that, do you think? Compared to the other gifts, healers are in small number in South Barrow."

Hamal shrugged. What he asked about was common knowledge. "Healers find easy employment in other barrows. There is no need for them to be poor." He thought of himself and shrugged again, a little self-consciously this time. "Well, most healers find easy employment." He was a little slow-witted. He knew this, and apparently, so did everyone who talked with him.

"Do you know what happens to the best healers, Hamal?"

"Good jobs in good houses?" Hamal suggested. He'd had a good job with Richart. Richart used to say that they were going to change modern healing methods with their research, but Hamal had no idea what happened to their research after Richart's death.

Cale thought about it. "Yes, a little bit. But in those houses, they serve as bodyguards and hold an elevated status among the regular private guard. If the private guard fail to keep the lord safe during an attack, the bodyguards are there to step in and save the lord's life. The more talented the healer, the closer he—or she, at times—is placed to the king. Would you take such a job if it were offered to you, Hamal?"

"Yes. I want to work."

"What if that job were with the king?"

Hamal's caution suddenly became a tangible element, something he could touch. "Wait, Cale. Do you mean...a soldier? A soldier for the king?" He felt his lips twitch. He tried not to laugh, because the idea was *laughable*, and if he started laughing, he might not be able to stop. Hamal, a soldier for the king? *Hamal?* After he had lived for two years in South Barrow? "Thank you for the offer, but I don't think I could do that."

Cale did not appear disturbed at Hamal's refusal. He watched him with his probing silver eyes and asked eventually, "Why not?"

"I am a healer. I don't want to hurt people."

Cale's eyes shut and opened in a slow blink. "You would be guarding the king, Hamal. That is a position that heals. You wouldn't hurt people. You would save a person—an important person."

Hamal shook his head. "I'm sorry, Cale, but I can't be a soldier for the king."

"Why not?"

It seemed that Cale did not often hear people tell him no. Hamal replied, "The king's soldiers have destroyed many families in South Barrow. Cally? You remember Cally?" When Cale silently nodded, Hamal explained, "She lost her husband a month ago. The soldiers came and arrested a large group of flamemakers—and weathermakers, too—and sold them across the river."

Hamal shook his head. "I can't do that. I like you, Cale. And I think you're brave. I am loyal to the king, but I can't take people away from their families. That does not bring healing. It just makes South Barrow angry. It makes it poorer than it was, and it hurts many people."

Cale, Mercen, and Rhyan exchanged long looks.

"Hamal," Cale said, "Cedrick's father abolished slavery ten years ago. Comparatively speaking, it was the sole point of controversy in his reign. His ruling on slavery altered the economy and created much upheaval in the kingdom."

Those last words were calmly spoken, but with his hand still pinned to Cale's chest, Hamal felt the sudden storm of pain that roared through the man's body. It raged. It fired. It was angry and hurt. And then, as quick as a blink, it ended, and Hamal didn't feel it anymore. But he knew. He knew it as clearly as he had known it in the tunnel, when Cale had been speaking to Rizen and the sadness flickered through his silver eyes. Cale had suffered loss. Something horrible had happened to Cale. He bore the pain strongly.

But there was no pain in his voice as he said gently, "No one has been bought and sold in the nation of King's Barrow in ten years. It is against the law. What are you talking about, Hamal?"

Hamal, surprised, tried to draw his hand away from Cale's chest, but Cale wouldn't let it go. He held it against him, as if he had seen healers do this in the past—read a man's body, feel what that man felt. Not every healer knew how to read a man's bones and hear his heart in his blood. But Cale was a wealthy man—he lived in North Barrow, after all—and probably had spent time around the healers of the wealthy. The better the healer, the more likely he had a good position in a wealthy house.

"The king's soldiers come to put down the fighting," Hamal finally answered. "If they catch you, they take you across the river and sell you. Flamemakers. Weathermakers." He shrugged a shoulder—the shoulder not attached to the hand currently nailed to Cale's chest. "They leave the other gifts alone, I think, but then the others don't fight as much as flamemakers and weathermakers. They're mostly quiet. They certainly leave the feelers alone. No one wants the feelers, which is too bad, because feelers make cities."

Cale blinked at him.

"And no one wants the thievers either. But flamemakers are in high demand. That's what I've heard people say. Everyone wants to buy flamemakers across the river. So the soldiers come and arrest you for fighting, if they can catch you, and then they take you and sell you, and no one ever sees your face again."

Surprise flickered through Cale's body. He turned his head and looked at Mercen.

The first lord stepped forward. He stood quite close to Hamal, and it felt awkward. "You are certain of this, Hamal?" His dark eyes narrowed. "I am not sure of your ability to remember what is true and then tell me in a way that is believable. You seem an overtly simple...boy."

Cale shot Mercen a frown, but Hamal could hardly be offended. He was a simple boy. If Mercen could tell, that meant Mercen was intelligent.

Hamal nodded. "The flamemakers have been reduced by half. At least by half. There used to be many of them, but their men and women are taken, and the children run about alone. You could speak to any of the flamemakers in South Barrow and hear again what I am telling you now. They avoid the king's men almost as strongly as they avoid weathermakers. The king's men come and make arrests."

"He speaks the truth, my lord," Cale said, looking toward Hamal with intense silver eyes.

Did he know what he was doing right now by holding Hamal's hand to his chest? Hamal could access his blood and bones; they were files of information he knew how to read. He was learning Cale's history—*Cale's* information. Cale, who hadn't told him anything about himself, but now he was forcing Hamal to learn anyway. Hamal tugged his hand, trying one more time for escape, but Cale kept him captive.

For a moment, the room was quiet.

"Someone has been helping himself to the city's poor," Rhyan murmured.

His father heaved a hot sigh and said, "That is just what we need. We have enough problems with South Barrow—the last thing the king needs is someone actively working against him to draw up the walls of defense."

Cale didn't say a word. After a while, Rhyan and Mercen both quieted and they watched him, waiting to hear what he would say.

"Justice," Cale said.

"Of what nature?" Mercen demanded.

"There is no justice in South Barrow," Cale said.

He loosened his grip, and Hamal pulled his hand away from Cale's chest, relieved. He didn't think Cale really wanted him to know his secrets. Cale seemed secretive.

"Hamal," Cale said.

Hamal looked at him.

"The throne does not own slaves. Cedrick is a good and faithful king, and he adheres to his father's regulations. It is not the king who has arrested your friends. Those soldiers in South Barrow—they are not the king's men. We will speak to the king about this, settle the matter, and bring those people home. All your friends. You have my word that this will be a problem quickly corrected."

"On top of everything else we're attempting to correct right now," Mercen muttered sourly.

7 The Bone Speech

They were in the middle of what Cale called a "quick supper"—it was more food and more *types* of food than Hamal had seen since Richart's house—when Cale suddenly stopped talking. His head turned abruptly, and he looked through the floor, as if it weren't there. When he used his seer eyes, it was as if everything melted away around him, and he could see what he wanted to see, even if it was far away.

The room was large, nearly as large as the entire South Barrow mission. It was amazing to Hamal how *big* things were in North Barrow. The walls were covered with beautiful tapestries. A rich carpet the color of sand concealed the floor. Hamal was almost afraid to walk on it for fear of getting it dirty with his boots. His boots had holes—they were dirty. Cale didn't seem to notice the wealth around them.

He said across the table, "The king is here."

His expression was odd, so Hamal asked, "Do you want to go see him?"

The silver eyes narrowed as Cale seemed to peer through the floor. "Masly is with him."

"Masly?"

Cale was easy to understand. He worded things simply. "The seer from the Kladis Tunnel. Remember? The man I do not trust."

Hamal remembered. Forgetfulness was not why he had spoken the man's name. Tension tightened his spine. "Why is a bad man with the king?"

With a sigh, Cale set his fork aside and turned a silver scowl at all the food set before them. "Oh, he is likely still looking for a body."

Hamal asked tentatively, "Your body?"

"Yes. And because he hasn't found it, I think he intends to talk the king into arresting the Kanyan lords on the *rumor* of my death, nothing more."

"But they didn't kill you!"

Cale glanced at him and smirked. "A brilliant observation."

Hamal grinned. He couldn't help it. Cale made him laugh. "Does the king believe Masly?"

"No." Cale shrugged. "But not accepting the word of a seer is a difficult task, especially when the rest of the government takes him quite seriously. Masly is, indeed, what Lord Mercen declared him to be—a most talented seer. A seer's word may not hold up without proof in the Court of Justice, but as seers, we expect to be heard and believed. Masly has been serving the throne since childhood. Most of the government believes him to be what he seems—quite trustworthy. He often travels with the king."

Hamal considered Cale's words. He looked at the food on the table and then at the fork in his hand and tried to think. "Will the king arrest the lords?"

Again Cale shrugged. "No. The rumors of my death at the hands of the House of Kanyan are meant to divide the king from his trusted friends. He knows who his friends are. But that doesn't mean he will act stupidly and ignore the rumor either."

Hamal had no idea what that meant.

"Depending on how things go, Mercen may bring the king up here, and if he does, you will get that meeting with him sooner than I promised."

They continued eating, Hamal keeping an eye on Cale, and eventually, Cale's fork lowered and met the tabletop. He leaned back in his chair.

"They're coming," he said, looking intently toward the door. "You may answer any of the king's questions, Hamal, but if Masly is still with him, look to me first. I will tell you whether or not you should answer him." A pause and then, "Masly may try to trick you."

Hamal nearly dropped his fork. "Why?"

Cale smiled at him. "Because he is looking for a body, and you graciously ruined his plans. He will want to know who you are—"

"And you don't want anyone to know who I am."

"Exactly. So just look to me, Hamal, and I will tell you if it's all right to answer a question. I will nod my head to you."

Hamal couldn't eat anymore after those words. He felt the tension like a cramp in his side.

A short time later—it felt like a very short time to Hamal—the door swung open, and a group of men entered the room.

The first man was upset. His heart beat in a rapid pattern that suggested anger and perhaps fear. He thundered into the room and halted, staring at Cale as he rose from the table.

"Your majesty," Cale said solemnly and bowed low.

The king. This was the king. Hamal looked at the man with interest. He appeared to be around thirty years old, but there was a little gray in his dark hair, and he had a nose like a hatchet, a triangular wedge that jutted off his face. Hamal doubted that many women found him handsome, yet he somehow looked like a king. Something about him seemed powerful. Hamal thought he could almost *feel* the man's strength, even from across the room.

As the king's gaze met Cale's, Hamal heard the beat of the king's heart grow calm, the emotions dropping back to normalcy. The king smiled, and Hamal noticed that when he smiled, his nose didn't seem as big.

Three men accompanied the king into the room. Two were the lords of Kanyan, and the third had a very fast heart. Hamal could hear the sharp staccato without effort. The beat did not alter as the man's gaze swept the room, clamped onto Cale, and seemed to dig into him.

The man's narrowed eyes were silver.

This had to be Masly.

Hamal remembered his manners—why was he always forgetting his manners?—and quickly stood up. No one seemed to notice him, but he still bowed on his side of the table anyway, as Cale had done. As he straightened, he caught sight of guards out in the hallway—men with hard faces and silver armor. *Many* guards. Concern twinged through him.

But he was here with Cale. And he believed what Cale told him, which meant everything would be all right.

Someone shut the door, and the room seemed to grow smaller as it was sealed from the hallway. Hamal could hear Masly's heart like a drum.

"Mercen," the king said, "I suppose you'll be keeping your head after all."

"Thank you, Sire."

His words were harsh, but the king hadn't lost his smile. Hamal looked at him more closely. What was his gift—was he a grower? Cedrick's family had held the throne for generations, and sometimes the gift changed, depending on whom the king married. Most kings were growers; they wanted to take care of the land and the people and help the nation flourish. Growers produced growers, as long as they married other growers. But if a grower married a jeweler, for instance, then the child might be a jeweler, and jewelers cared more about making money and prospering financially than they did about building the land and the people. They weren't bad kings; they just tended to be a little less pleasant, yet the treasury always prospered in their keeping. A jeweler for a king meant a rich nation.

Hamal felt eyes prodding his skin. Cold slid down his spine and popped up chill bumps on his arms. Masly was looking at him.

The king folded his arms. "I want the story, Cale. What happened?"

This time, Cale told the story. He didn't look at Hamal and hardly mentioned him, except to say that Hamal was a healer who worked at the mission.

Hamal recognized the telling of a secret. Cale had been much more open with Mercen and Rhyan than he was now with the king. He gave only a few of the details, a handful of them, and as the story progressed, Hamal again grew aware of Masly's pointed gaze. It felt uncomfortable. He wanted to shrug it off, like a coat that didn't fit him properly.

The king looked at Hamal. "Thank you for the role you played in saving this man's life."

A flush soared through Hamal's face. Not knowing what else to do, he bowed again, and Cale started to smile, which made Hamal's blush all the worse. He barely knew anything about kings! Everyone was watching him, and he wondered what he had done wrong. The room was quiet now, more than before, and for a brief moment, he wondered why he could no longer hear Masly's heartbeat. It occurred to him that the man had calmed.

Masly spoke for the first time. "We expected you at the palace, Cale," he said in a voice that was as soft and airy as Rhyan's was deep and booming. This was not the voice of an orator. Masly sounded like a child.

Whiny, Hamal realized. *He sounds whiny.*

"I wager I am still expected at the palace," Cale replied.

"Why did you not return to us sooner? Why come here? It is a…relief to see you alive."

Hamal's brows drew together. The king had been relieved. Lord Mercen had been relieved. But when Masly had seen Cale, the beat of his heart hadn't been one of joy or happiness. And he sounded so…young. Hamal had healed a throat or two in his lifetime; idly, he wondered if this problem with Masly's voice was something that could be healed, or if he had been born this way. Sometimes the gods gave strange gifts to men, like peculiar voices. When it was a gift of the gods, it could not be changed.

"Your concern is moving," Cale replied softly.

A muscle twitched below Masly's eye. His hard silver gaze flicked to Hamal, who took a step back as it touched him. "And who are you?"

Hamal swallowed as he remembered what Cale had said. *I will tell you whether or not you should answer him.*

"He is a healer," Cale replied easily. "Hamal, why don't you tell Masly what it is like to work at the mission? Your majesty, if I may speak to you in private for a moment?"

Hamal just stared at him. In private? The mission? The words didn't make sense. Cale was leaving him alone with Masly? His mouth suddenly felt dry, as if he'd been chewing on dead grass. Cale and the king retreated to a distant corner of the room, and Mercen went with them, as if he thought they expected him to follow. For a brief moment, Hamal stood there alone with Masly.

But then Rhyan shifted position, moving forward to join them. The second lord of Kanyan took a position to Hamal's right, and he folded his arms and spent a good deal of time studying Masly as Hamal stuttered through a description of the mission. The words were hard to say at first, but then it felt like his tongue loosened, and he told Masly everything he could think of. He gave him the mission's history and told him, in detail, about the fire they'd had in the kitchen that one time. He told him about the gangrenous foot and the boy who fell off the steps of the bakery and broke his arm. Masly heard all about old Mrs. Felster, who had only one eye but was very good at healing eyes. And fingers. For some reason, she was very good at healing fingers as well.

"And are you a good healer, Hamal?" Masly asked in his little boy's voice.

Hamal shrugged. "I am a good healer, but I am not great. I leave scars. I don't know how to heal without scars."

Masly's silver eyes strayed to Cale, who was speaking quietly with the king. Hamal had excellent hearing, but even he couldn't hear a word out of that corner. The three men standing there were as quiet as a painting.

"They never let me have any of the hard cases at the mission," Hamal said, wanting to draw Masly's gaze away from the corner. "But once, I got to heal a toe. The man had stubbed it on a door. He was running barefoot, and then he didn't come to the mission for a week, so his toe was swollen and infected, and it was the size of a…"

The silver eyes came back around.

Hamal swallowed under their weight. "I healed the toe."

"Why is this important?" Masly asked.

Hamal rubbed the top of his head and didn't know what to tell him. He knew he wasn't a good storyteller. "I don't really like toes," he finished and felt his shoulders sinking toward the floor.

"Masly," the king called from across the room, much to Hamal's relief.

Masly nodded to Lord Rhyan. "Excuse me, my lord," he said politely, but Hamal he completely ignored. It was like those silver eyes couldn't even see him anymore.

Hamal nearly lost his footing as he scrambled to get out of the seer's way. As Masly headed toward the corner, his shoulder brushed Hamal's—a light brush, no more than a tap, but it was enough. The rest of the room seemed to fade from Hamal's sight. The floor at his feet, the sensation of losing his balance—everything seemed to pause as he heard the shout of Masly's bones. Bones were books. Books of information. The touch of Masly's shoulder to his was short and clipped, but Hamal could feel that Masly was in agony. Hamal had never felt this kind of pain in another man. The bones seemed to scream at him, desperate for salvation. How could the man seem so calm and in control? His bones were screaming.

Then Hamal found his footing. The room righted itself. Sounds and movement returned to their proper balance.

"Pardon, my lord," he whispered as Masly strode away. Hamal stared after him. His heart was racing—Hamal's heart. Rhyan had to speak to him a few times before Hamal finally registered the sound of his voice. He blinked at the flamemaker. "My lord? I'm sorry. I…" The words stopped.

Rhyan studied him. He glanced at Masly's back and then leaned forward, asking quietly, "Hamal, are you quite all right?"

"Yes," Hamal answered. He was fine. Masly was not.

"You must forgive me, Hamal, for I do not know much about healers. I know that skilled healers can touch a man and know what ails his body, but some can do even more than that. Some can even *read* a man's bones. Is this true?"

Hamal nodded mutely. It was an easy thing to do, to touch a person and read the body. *Bones are books.* His heart pounded rapidly.

"Did you just read Masly?" Rhyan's brows rose up his forehead. "Your face turned a peculiar shade of green."

Hamal shuddered.

Masly was speaking with the king. He was shaking his head, disagreeing, but the voices were still so low that Hamal couldn't hear them. He suddenly became aware of Cale's eyes upon him from across the room. He could feel the touch, just as he could feel Masly's, yet Cale was different than Masly. Cale's gaze almost felt gentle; Hamal knew Cale and he knew he was kind. Masly's gaze felt like sharp, cold stones. Hamal was starting to think he knew Masly, too.

"What did you see?" Rhyan whispered.

"He's sick. He's so sick. I don't even know how he's standing. He feels an incredible amount of pain. He is *ill*." Hamal had felt similar things in others so he knew what he was feeling this time, but the *strength* of it in Masly was like a punch in the stomach. All the air left Hamal's lungs, and he didn't know how to respond.

Rhyan's gaze never left Hamal's face. After a moment, he sighed with displeasure and said, "I suppose the right course of action would be to send you to heal him."

"No."

The dark brows rose up the forehead again. "No?"

"I can't heal Masly. This isn't something a healer can fix."

Again, the solid stare. The flamemaker shook his head once. "I don't understand." The brows lowered now. "You healed Cale of a mortal wound. You did the impossible, Hamal. You did what no other healer could have done. Why can you not heal Masly?"

Rhyan didn't make sense. Many of his words rolled about in the air and never came to form. They were like clouds. Hamal couldn't touch clouds, could he? He didn't know what Rhyan was talking about. And he didn't know how to explain to him what he meant about Masly. What the lord was obviously thinking—it wasn't right. "Masly does not have an illness."

A pause. "But you just said he is sick."

"It is not a natural sickness. He's in pain in his bones. It is...it is a sickness of emotion. If the emotion is strong enough, a healer can feel it in the body. Masly thinks he has done wrong, and the guilt is written in his bones like words." Hamal sucked in a breath, remembering what he had felt. "He is so very sick—with guilt. Guilt seeps down into the bones and stays there. It hurts the bones. It stays with the body."

Gradually, he became aware that the beat of Rhyan's heart had increased. Rhyan asked calmly, "What happened, Hamal?" The words were low.

"I don't know. But it hurts him."

"Can you…can you tell the *age* of the guilt?"

Hamal peered up at him. "What do you mean?"

Impatience flickered through the flamemaker's eyes, but it left quickly. It seemed he didn't *want* to be impatient with Hamal, but he really couldn't help it, could he? He was a flamemaker. Flamemakers were always just a little impatient. "Was it—the bad thing—something he did long ago, or did it happen recently?"

Oh. The *age* of the guilt. Hamal nodded. "The bones speak loudly. It is recent guilt, I think. Something within the last several months."

A long breath of air rolled out of Rhyan's lungs. "Thank you, Hamal. You have done well." He said nothing more.

They waited for the king to finish with his seers. The quiet conversation in the corner lasted several more minutes.

Masly was frowning, his silver eyes narrow. Eventually, the king held up a hand. Loudly, so even Hamal could hear, he said, "Keep your peace, Masly. You've heard my final word on the subject."

Masly bowed his head once, giving in.

Cedrick put his back to the corner and walked across the carpet to Rhyan and Hamal. The seers and Mercen followed in silence. Mercen's face was red, but his smile seemed pleased. Hamal hoped his pleased look meant that Cale was right and the king still wasn't going to kill the first lord of Kanyan.

Cedrick stopped in front of Hamal and folded his arms. Tilting his head back to look down his very large nose and said, "I understand you're interested in working for me."

"If it pleases you, your majesty."

"I've decided it does."

And just like that, Hamal was off the streets.

8 The House of Red Stone

The king left with Masly, and a short time later, Hamal and Cale took one of the Kanyan coaches to another grand house on another street. This house was made of stones that looked like fire. Granted, a dull sort of fire, Hamal thought, but it was a unique color. And he would wager it was expensive.

"Where are we?" he asked Cale.

The seer had been quiet for the duration of the journey, his head back against the seat, his silver eyes closed. He sat up at Hamal's question and glanced out the window. "This is my father's house," he answered quietly.

"Oh," Hamal said. "He will like that you are alive."

A corner of Cale's mouth pulled in. "My father has been dead for five years. I live here. The house came to me." Cale paused. He reached up and rubbed the thumb of his damaged right hand across his eyes. "The house in Brannack went to my brother. My mother lives with him."

This was Cale's home. Hamal slid to the edge of the seat and peered through the window with interest. It made sense that the house had come to Cale by blood and that he hadn't built it himself. Cale didn't seem like a red-stone house sort of man. "Is he a seer, too?"

"Who?"

"Your brother with the house in Brannack."

Cale blinked at him slowly. "No. He is a grower, like our parents."

"Which family member was the seer?" The seer gift didn't act like the other gifts; it didn't follow a pattern in a man's bloodline but jumped around. One child might be a seer, and then that child's grandson might be the next seer.

"My great-grandmother," Cale replied.

Ah, so it was a distant relative then, Hamal thought. *A distant relation.* He wondered if anyone had been surprised when Cale was born a seer instead of a grower like the rest of his family.

Seers were interesting, and they rarely married other seers. Hamal didn't know why. He supposed it might be odd for *two* people to know so much about one another, each of them seeing into the other. Perhaps it would be happier for only one to know so much and for the other to be a different gift, like a grower. Growers tended to be gentle people; they knew about working the earth and caring for it. Cale's father must have been a very talented man to afford a house like this one.

The coach stopped at the base of a large staircase, and a well-dressed servant opened the coach's door. The man saw Cale's face, and his eyes widened. He sucked in a breath. "My lord!"

Cale greeted the servant by name, as well as the guards on the steps, and took Hamal inside, where Hamal was more surprised than ever. Cale's house made the Kanyan house look like a home in South Barrow. This was a palace. Hamal's jaw dropped.

Seeing his face, Cale glanced through the large entry and said with a frown, "My mother is fond of silver."

Hamal couldn't help but think that her favorite color matched

Cale's eyes. She must like looking at her son.

"And rubies," Cale added. "Silver and rubies."

Hamal had no idea what rubies would match, except blood, but he doubted that was the mother's reasoning. Roses perhaps?

Every servant they saw showed visible signs of relief that Cale was all right. Hamal heard running steps, and more servants appeared. Most just watched. Several of the women wiped tears. Cale's steps slowed as he saw all the faces, all the people who had mourned him, thinking he was dead.

Cale said nothing more until they entered a sitting room of sorts. Hamal had no idea where they were in the house—somewhere on the second floor—but didn't mind not knowing. He knew now more than ever that saving Cale's life had been a good idea. *Look at all the people who love him.*

The sitting room was comfortable, and it looked like Cale in ways the rest of the house did not. It was rather plain, with brown couches, a black rug, and dark curtains that didn't let in the light. *A seer's sitting room,* Hamal thought, looking around, *when he doesn't wish to see anything.*

Servants brought in trays of food. Cale thanked them and didn't say a word about all the food they had just eaten at the House of Kanyan. Hamal's eyes widened as the table in the center of the room filled to overflowing. Servant after servant entered and exited, many of them bringing food, but some apparently came just to catch a glimpse of Cale, as if to assure themselves the stories were true and he lived. In the midst of the crowd came a young woman. She wasn't wearing the same red-and-brown garments as the servants, but her clothing was just as simple. She was quite pretty, Hamal thought, with smooth features and thick dark hair, but it was her large eyes that held Hamal's interest the most. The irises were clouded and murky. She was blind.

Cale smiled when he saw her. "Satha," he said, and she turned toward the sound of his voice.

"Cale." Her hand lifted.

He came off the couch and touched her raised hand with his. Her shoulders lowered as a sigh rolled from her, and her clouded eyes closed with relief. Hamal saw the muscles move in her throat as she swallowed.

She released another breath. "Are you all right?" Her voice was strangely calm.

"Yes."

"Is it true? This rumor that you were attacked?"

"Yes." He met the servants' gazes, and without any other signal, they left the room, the door closing silently behind them. "Satha," he said when they were alone, "this is Hamal. He is a healer."

"He is the one who saved your life?" She still spoke calmly. She seemed like a very calm person.

"He did."

Cale put his hands on the woman's shoulders and gently turned her toward Hamal. Her hands rose again, and Hamal, who had spent time with the blind, stepped forward and gripped them.

"Thank you, Hamal," she said, still calm, but her voice was lower now. She squeezed his hands, and he noted that she had a strong grip. "You have spared me much pain."

Hamal knew why Cale's death would have hurt her. Her blood told him. "Cale is the bravest man I know," he replied happily. "You're very welcome."

In those few moments as she held his hands, he heard the voice of her bones, the history keepers of a person's body. She had a disease. In her eyes. It had begun in the womb, clouding her vision when she was just a small child, and she had been completely blind by the time she was seven.

Her bones told him several other things as well—she was a seer. Like Cale. The disease cloaked the true color of her eyes, so you couldn't tell what she was. In most cases, Hamal could not touch a person and know that person's gift. He hadn't known that Cale was a seer until the man had opened his eyes, but Hamal knew Satha's gift because of the way it was hindered by the disease. The eyes were very important for all the gifts. Sometimes when a man lost his eyes, either through sickness or age, he lost his gift as well. That happened perhaps fifty percent of the time.

Cale loved Satha and looked after her. Surely, he had brought healers to see her. He worked for the king—perhaps Cale had even met Richart, Hamal's old friend, and Richart had been a talented healer. Why, then, was Satha still blind? It was just a disease. Hamal and Richart had talked about disease in detail, and they used to say that it was like having rats in the stable. Yes, it caused problems, but in the end it was possible to get rid of rats. You could fix the problem. It didn't really matter what the disease was—just get rid of the rats.

In the quiet, Cale said, "Satha is visiting from Brannack. She is a good friend of my mother's and comes down several times a year. She..." The words ebbed. He took a shallow breath and said, "She is my wife."

Satha's head came around, and she looked toward Cale in obvious surprise.

"I know," Hamal replied.

Cale blinked slowly. "How do you know?"

Hamal let go of Satha's hands. She stood there a moment, hands extended, then slowly lowered them.

"Her blood told me." And, because Cale had expressed interest in the past, Hamal explained, "The blood always knows its mate. That is why it is good to have only one mate—so as not to confuse the blood. Confused blood makes a person unhealthy." He nodded as he thought about it and then said something that interested him: "You and Satha are unique, you know."

"In what way?" Cale asked.

"Well, seers don't often marry each other…I don't know why. Maybe it's because there are so few seers, and they don't find each other. The gift doesn't follow a predictable pattern, you know, the way other gifts do. The seer gift will eventually produce other seer gifts, but it might not be among that man's children. It might be in his grandchildren, or his nieces and nephews. Hard to say."

Hamal shrugged and then remembered his point. "But whenever seers do get married to one another, they don't have babies who are seers; they have babies who are prophets. Two seer gifts together produce the prophet's gift. I don't know why that is either. King's Barrow hasn't had a prophet in a very long time. They have golden eyes, you know—prophets do. Seers are silver, but prophets are gold. It's very pretty, actually. It looks nice."

Neither Cale nor his wife said a word, so after a quiet moment, Hamal shifted uncomfortably and continued, "Prophets are scary. They are brash, like flamemakers, but they know things. They like to tell you what's going to happen to you, even if you don't want them to. But you will be a good father, Cale, so I think your prophets will be good, too. Good daughters. Good sons—kind ones. I know a prophet, and I like him very much. So it is possible for a prophet to be kind, if he has the right parents."

Hamal realized that Satha was gripping her hands together so hard that her knuckles were turning white.

"Satha is a seer?" Cale asked quietly.

Hamal looked at him in shock. "Cale! *You're* a seer. Don't you know what your wife is?"

"I do not see everything." He stared at Hamal, blinked slowly, and then glanced at the closed study door as if remembering something. "And no one knows Satha is my wife. It is a secret. I told you so you would know how grateful I am for what you did for us." He stopped. "She is a seer?"

Hamal felt his forehead wrinkling. Why would anyone keep his wife a secret? Surely, North Barrow was a curious place, with curious ways of living.

"Cale…" Satha whispered. "Oh, Cale."

Cale drew in an unsteady breath. "She has been to healers all her life, Hamal. Ever since she was a very little child. No one has been able to do anything for her."

Hamal fully expected one more sentence to follow. He expected a request. He could practically see the words on Cale's face, but the seer kept the request to himself and did so for several hours. He did so all through dinner, not breathing a word or even the suggestion of it. He did not ask even as the servants cleared the dishes away.

The three of them—Cale, Satha, and Hamal—were alone in a sitting room on the first floor sipping hot cups of honeyed tea when Cale finally couldn't seem to contain himself anymore.

"Hamal," he began, setting his cup aside. "Normally I would not ask this. You are a guest in my home. I would not treat you as anything less than a guest, an honored guest, but I have a…a question."

Hamal nodded. "You want me to heal your wife."

Cale paused.

So did Satha. Her cup of tea suddenly seemed pinned to her chin.

Shifting awkwardly, Cale said, "I would like you to look at her, if you are willing."

"Of course I am willing, Cale! You are my friend. You could ask me anything." Putting his cup down on the short table in front of the couch, Hamal stood up and explained, "Some people are a little funny about healers. Take the Theranians, for instance. Once outside the city of Riverstone, I came upon a cart accident, and the man didn't want me to heal him. Theranians don't like to be touched by outsiders, you know. Instead, he preferred to just sit there in agony until one of his own healers arrived."

Hamal walked over to Satha where she sat in a large padded chair with red roses stitched into the fabric. "Then there was this other time when I knew I could heal a man with a bad knee, so I healed him—and he was angry! Apparently, a rich man had hurt the knee in a hunting accident years before, and every month the rich man sent the injured man a stipend. So he wanted to keep the hurt knee so he wouldn't have to work. It was all very strange, but since then, I've always asked before I healed people."

Cale didn't seem to be listening. "You..." He started over. "You think you can actually...do something?"

Heal her. He couldn't even say the words.

Hamal took the cup of tea from Satha's hands and put it on the table next to his own cup. With careful, gentle movements so he wouldn't startle her, he put his hands on her face.

This disease was not common. He had, actually, never come across it before, and it made him miss Richart. Richart would have loved examining Satha; he had greatly enjoyed studying things he did not understand, and this disease would have enthralled him. It was unique, but Hamal knew it would not be difficult for him to heal because the eyes were not dead; they were simply blocked.

Leaning forward, he adjusted his touch and put one finger to her forehead. The disease was wrapped through the tissue of each eye, front to back, and a little pressure was all it took to begin to unravel it. He pushed once and felt the bonds break apart.

Beneath his hand, Satha began to blink at him with large silver eyes.

"Hello," Hamal greeted. ,

Cale's wife sat in his lap and touched his face as if she were still blind, her fingertips making friends with his cheekbones, his eyes, his nose, his lips. She didn't have a significant visible reaction the way some people did when given good gifts. Her reaction was quiet and internal, but it seemed to Hamal that Cale heard every word. The man didn't stop smiling. Half an hour passed, and the smile didn't fade a single time. Not a twitch. He watched her, Hamal completely forgotten.

When she finally spoke, her voice was soft. "I could always tell when you were looking at me." Her fingers paused on the sides of his face. "That is how I fell in love with you. Because I could feel your stare, and you stared all the time."

Hamal didn't mind being forgotten by friends who were happy. Sitting on the couch, he twiddled his thumbs and started thinking about what it would be like to work for the king. He imagined it would be very different than working for Richart and doing research with him. Why wasn't anyone supposed to know that Cale was married to this woman? He so obviously loved her.

"Hamal."

Hamal lifted his head. Cale wasn't looking at him; he was looking at his wife.

"Satha is the king's cousin, and I am not a nobleman. Technically, it is against the law for me to be married to her."

"I care about laws even less than I did a few minutes ago," Satha replied.

"How can you not be a nobleman?" Hamal asked. "Look at your house!"

Cale laughed once. It wasn't a happy laugh, but it didn't sound very sad either. "There is a difference between having money and being born a nobleman. My father and his father before him did very well for themselves, but that does not make us a noble house. If Cedrick learns of our union, it is possible Satha will lose her title."

"It is possible the king will be in a mood to be persuaded," Satha said softly.

Here, for the first time since Satha's eyes turned silver, Cale's smile became less pronounced. He began to look sad. "We've talked about this, my heart."

She looked over his face one more time and said almost lazily, "Perhaps you should see what I see."

And Cale, for some reason, turned absolutely scarlet.

Satha giggled. "And you, my heart, must understand me. We concealed our union for more than one reason. It might have caused you to lose your position with the prince." The words grew soft. "But the prince is dead, and even if the king cannot be persuaded to allow me to keep my title and my position in his house…" She smiled, and her fingers tracked a path through his hair. "I can see your face."

She leaned forward and kissed him, and Hamal looked away. Just for a moment. She continued speaking after a short time.

"I can see your face. And I find I no longer require the king's house."

"Satha—"

"Hush. You're about to find me more stubborn than you've ever found me in the past."

Again, scarlet swept Cale's face. A swift and ferocious fire. Why the blush? Hamal did not understand it.

9 The Body in the Well

The next morning, Cale took Hamal to the king's palace. It was a large, sprawling structure everyone called the *Hoagaran*, an old word meaning "justice." To Hamal's untrained eyes, it resembled a city within a city, and he sensed the great number of times he was about to get lost in its hallways.

He could feel Cale's eyes on him.

"Hamal," Cale finally said from the other side of the coach, "you will not be able to trust anyone in the palace. You know this, don't you?"

"I will be able to trust Leelah," Hamal replied.

Another slow blink. "Who is Leelah?"

"Richart's daughter."

Cale just stared at him for a moment. "She…works at the palace?"

"Yes."

The coach stopped at a secondary gate. The captain of the guard who peered through their window wore armor that glinted in the early morning sunlight, and he clearly knew who Cale was. He glanced at Cale and Hamal and didn't ask them their names or business before waving the driver forward.

"Hamal," Cale said as the coach began to roll forward again. "Richart Sangren had three sons. He did not have any daughters."

Hamal nodded. "Leelah's mother was not Richart's wife." He shrugged and rubbed at his nose with the back of his wrist. "In Richart's home, no one was supposed to talk about Leelah, but she is a healer, too, and Richart helped her find work at the palace. I think she still works there."

After a moment, Cale said calmly, "Richart's daughter, illegitimate or not, would have been given special treatment, Hamal. I know many of the healers who work in the palace, and none of them is named *Leelah*."

"I haven't seen her in years," Hamal replied. "Perhaps she has found work elsewhere. She is intelligent, like her father. It would be easy for her to find work."

The coach rolled toward the main doors of the palace.

"Hamal."

"Yes?"

"If you say there is a healer named Leelah who works at the palace, and she is Richart's daughter, I believe you."

"She must have moved on," Hamal said.

Cale's brows rose slightly. "Perhaps," he replied.

When the coach stopped, Cale waited like the rich man he was, and servants appeared to open the doors. Hamal wasn't used to other men opening the doors for him. It made him feel off balance.

They were escorted by a single guard through a small door that was set far away from the main, well-guarded doors of the palace. This door was well guarded also, but again Cale's face was known. No one stopped them or asked their business. Hamal started to think that Cale must have spent a good deal of time here at the palace; the seer acted the same way here that he did in his home.

Three hallways, two doors, and a staircase later, Hamal found himself outside a row of offices. Each wooden door was shut, but they had nameplates on them. Cale stopped in front of the one that said *Meles Colbis*.

"This is the captain of the king's private guard," he told Hamal quietly. "He's expecting you."

Cale hesitated. He shifted position, folding his arms, and his elbow slid across Hamal's forearm. It was a brief, accidental touch, yet Hamal *felt* his hesitation. It was as if Cale's entire body were hesitating. Cale glanced at the soldier who had escorted them here, and the man turned and walked back up the stairs as if commanded audibly.

"Hamal," Cale said, "these are hard times for the country. They are hard for the king and his family. He has already suffered one great loss, so I think it is good that you work for him now. I think you will do well here, though it might be a difficult adjustment for you."

Cale frowned at the nameplate. "Should you change your mind and want to leave, feel free to tell me. I will speak to the king on your behalf."

"Do you work in the palace, too?" Hamal asked. "Will I get to see you all the time?"

The frown broke as Cale started smiling, but before he could reply, they heard boot steps on the stairs, and another soldier appeared. The man didn't come fully into the corridor; he stopped on the last step and said to Cale across the way, "Commander, the captain wants to see you in the Athos Well."

Hamal had no idea what an *athos well* was.

"Why?" Cale asked.

The soldier replied, "He has need of your abilities." He paused, glancing at Hamal. It was a processing look. "There was a body in the water."

The Athos Well was the deepest part of the palace—a circular space that was more like a giant shaft sunk into the earth than an actual room. Water rushed wildly just beneath a wide hole in the stone floor. Hamal could feel the spray as he stood nearby, quietly watching Cale and Captain Colbis examine the dead man.

A metal grate fixed around the base of the hole filtered the water and kept the Athos Well from being completely open to the river. Hamal could see the top of the slimy metal squares from where he stood. Cale had told him that the grate extended twenty feet into the bottom of the river, just in case any of the king's enemies thought to use the well as an entrance into the palace. The body had caught on the grate; a serving woman had seen the dead man's hand floating in the water. He had been fished out of the river and left to dry on the stone floor.

The body clearly had been in the river for several hours. The skin was discolored and bloated, and even without touching the man, Hamal could tell that he had lost a good deal of blood, though he could not see any obvious wounds. He grimaced as his stomach turned over. He did not like seeing death. What healer did? He could smell the river—the room smelled moldy.

"The river drowns dozens of people every year," the captain said. "You know protocol, Cale. This man worked for me, and I simply need to hear that this was an accident."

As Cale stared at the body, Hamal realized that Cale had done this before, maybe even many times. He had examined dead bodies for the king.

The seer was quiet for a time. "He entered the water between the Sixth and Fifth Bridges."

"How did it happen?" Colbis asked.

"I see him falling over the side of a barge."

The captain grunted. "No one observed his fall?"

Again, Cale was quiet, watching something only he could see. "I see crates and boxes. It appears to be a merchant vessel—from

Brannack. The city seal is clear on the railing, not far from where he fell. He was alone when he entered the water. No alarm was raised."

"An accident, then."

Cale hesitated. "Maybe."

Colbis' brows jerked together in a fierce frown. "Maybe? One of my men washes up in the palace, and you think it was *maybe* an accident? *Maybe* a murder?"

"I said *maybe*, and I did not use the word *murder*."

"Why are you suspicious of his death? Everything you reported just now seems to point toward an accident—no one was with him when he went in the water. For it to be an actual murder, wouldn't you see someone with him?"

Hamal looked at Cale in fascination. He could see all of that? He spoke these things like he could see them in pictures in his head, which made Hamal wonder if that was how the seer gift worked—pictures in the head. Perhaps Cale wouldn't mind if he asked him a few questions later.

Eventually, Cale noticed his stare and smiled slightly. "Do you concur, Master Healer?"

No one had ever called Hamal a master healer before. He laughed once, recognizing the joke. "I don't know what that means."

Cale reworded the question. "Do you think the death was accidental?"

Colbis looked at Cale a moment and then turned and looked at Hamal. "The king spoke of you. I am looking forward to meeting you somewhere else, where we can have a decent conversation. Nothing decent about this." He frowned down at the body in disgust, as if the man had died just to spite him. "If Cale calls a boy a master healer, then so do I." He murmured under his breath, "Even if that boy looks like he's barely old enough to hold a sword."

"I'm seventeen," Hamal replied helpfully.

The captain just stared at him.

"Hamal," Cale said, "I know you are familiar with the art of bone reading. What can you tell us about this man? Tell us everything you can about him, even if you think we won't find it important."

"Well, I can tell you his name and his gift and how he died. But you already know his name, and I suppose you already know his gift, too, since he worked for the captain."

When Cale and the captain didn't say anything, Hamal rubbed his nose and went on, "His name was Failan. He was a healer."

"Yes," Colbis said. "But how do you know he was a healer?"

"Well, I usually can't tell what a man's gift is just by his body alone, but I can always tell with a healer. I don't know why. We *feel* the same, I suppose. His name was Failan, and he was a healer, and he was dead before he entered the water."

Cale came alert. "How do you know?"

"Because of the loss of blood." Hamal crouched down beside the body and grasped the man's cold hand where it lay on the floor. Poor Failan had been dead for hours. "Bones are history keepers, you know. They remember strong emotions and sometimes even events, depending on what that event is."

Cale joined Hamal on the floor. "Such as the body's death."

"Exactly." Hamal smiled at him, pleased at his reply. "The last emotion this man felt before he died was helplessness. I think he was afraid and angry, too, but the main emotion was helplessness. I can feel it in his bones like a vibration. I know what I am feeling because I have felt it in bones before."

Colbis squatted down beside them. "Why would a healer feel helpless?"

"Well, he's dead. So it must have something to do with that."

Colbis rolled his eyes toward the roof.

"Can you answer the question in a different way, Hamal?" Cale asked. "What would cause a healer to feel helpless like this?"

"A healer feels helpless when he cannot do his job. I feel helpless, Cale, because I cannot heal your hand. Any healer who reads my bones would know I feel this way, because I feel it strongly. I wish I could make you fully well, and I can't make you fully well."

Colbis' head came up. He looked at Cale sharply. "So the rumors I've heard about you are true."

Cale waved him off. "What else, Hamal? Do you know what kept this man from being able to save his own life and heal himself?"

"I think so. Look." Hamal held up the dead man's hand, pulling down the hem of the tattered sleeve. "See the marks here? On his wrist?"

Cale leaned forward, as did Colbis. After a moment, Cale said, "You think he was bound first."

"Yes. Someone tied him up and then..." Hamal put the hand down gently and began to untie the dead man's tunic, near the throat. "The killing stroke was done somewhere on the neck. There should be a wound left over." Shifting position, he leaned over the body and examined the pale skin. "They cut his throat and then drained the blood until he died."

"But the clothes are new," Cale interjected. "There were never any bloodstains on these clothes. They changed his garments *after* he was killed."

"Why?" Colbis demanded.

Cale was quiet. "To conceal the cause of death."

"I don't understand," Hamal murmured, peering at the body. "His bones say this is how he died. There is no mistake. There should be a mark on the neck—they cut his throat and bled him. But there isn't a mark."

Cale released his breath slowly. "Because he was healed."

"What?" the captain demanded.

Despite the sounds of the water rushing through the grate, Hamal heard the sudden jump in Cale's heart. "They cut his throat, drained his blood—killed him, and then healed the neck, so we would be more likely to think the death an accidental drowning. They then arranged for the body to enter the river without human help, because they knew what a seer would be looking for to judge the cause of death."

Colbis hissed a low curse.

"You realize what this means, Captain. This man was killed by a healer. Or by someone working with a healer."

Hamal sucked in a sharp breath. A healer who killed? The notion was shocking. It wasn't right.

Colbis stood abruptly. "You make my job so much easier, Cale. I always appreciated that about you."

To Hamal's ears, the captain did not sound very appreciative at all.

Cale jumped to his feet. "You are upset—more than I was expecting. Why?"

Flashing him a scowl, Colbis dragged a hand through his close-cropped hair and said gruffly, "Because this is the second healer we've dragged out of the river this week, and both of them worked for me. I want you to look at the first body. Masly said it was an accident, and I'm hoping your healer agrees with him. The last thing I need right now is a patternmaker who is after the king's guards."

10 The Conversation in The Closet

"Cale," Hamal whispered as they strode down the hallway.

Cale glanced at him, brows lifted.

"I thought I knew all the gifts that could be known, but I don't know the gift the captain just said. What is a patternmaker?"

Quietly, the seer answered, "A patternmaker is not a gift. It is someone who kills for need or sport according to a certain pattern. Hence the name. He makes a pattern, and every person he kills follows that pattern. A few years ago, a patternmaker began killing off the lower-class merchants living in East Barrow. Not the rich men. The ones who hadn't been as successful as the rest. He killed only those who shipped by land, not by water, and only those who were gone from their households more than six months out of the year. It took us three months to stop him, and in the interim, he killed seven people in a specific way, following a specific pattern."

"Is this what you do for the king? You stop bad men?"

Again, Cale glanced at him. Hamal could feel his eyes.

"Sometimes, yes." For the rest of the walk to the holding chamber, Cale was silent.

The first body had been discovered two days ago. After Masly's examination, the body had been prepared by a healer, wrapped in cloths, and sealed within a casket for departure later in the week. The man's family lived in Brannack. He would be sent home with the king's guards as attendants, and the family would be well paid for their loss. Cale explained all of this to Hamal as the casket was opened carefully and the body revealed.

"The king protects and honors his dead," Cale finished.

As gently as he could, Hamal set his hand on the dead man's chest. Through the wrappings, the bones immediately began to speak to him, because they had something to say. Bones always spoke, no matter their age or how long the person had been dead.

Colbis shifted his weight in his boots. Then he shifted again, folding his arms. Hamal felt pressure building in the captain's body. He didn't have to touch him to know what was going on.

"Well?" the captain eventually asked.

"This man died by drowning," Hamal said.

"Good," Colbis replied.

Hamal made a face. "But it's…his body is not quite right."

Cale took a step closer to the table where the open casket sat. "What do you mean, Hamal?"

Hamal sighed and hoped he could find the right words. He wasn't always good with his words. "This man felt helpless at the moment of his death."

Colbis nodded, the motion impatient. Hamal could hear the tension in the pulse of the captain's heart. "I imagine that most men who drown feel that way."

"Yes, but it's not right. The blood is confused."

"Confused?" Cale repeated. "This man felt confused?"

"No, *he* felt helpless. His *blood* felt confused. There is a difference, you know. When the blood is confused, it means that something in the body is not functioning as it should be. That is, something is keeping the body from functioning as it should."

Colbis muttered a curse and asked, "Like ropes?"

"No. This man wasn't tied up." Hamal withdrew his hand and looked down at the body sadly. "I think he swallowed something that shut his body down."

The captain started frowning again.

So Hamal explained, "He drowned because he couldn't move. The blood was confused—why couldn't he move? The blood can become confused with certain types of medications because it doesn't understand why the rest of the body is responding the way it is."

"He was poisoned," Cale stated.

"I don't know if it was poison," Hamal replied slowly. "It wasn't necessarily a bad medication—it was just something that made him unable to swim."

The captain and Cale looked at one another.

"Two of my men in three days," Colbis said. He suddenly sounded tired, though his heart was still racing. Hamal could hear it.

"Three," Hamal said and then blushed as the men looked at him.

"Hamal," Cale began patiently. "What are you thinking?"

The captain had far less patience. "What do you mean *three*?" he demanded.

"Well…" Hamal shifted uncomfortably, drawing back a step from the casket. "And Cale. Aren't you counting Cale? I thought you would count Cale."

Again, the captain and Cale looked at one another. Cale quietly told the captain a few details from the night he met Hamal.

"Completely different method of attack and disposal," Colbis said. "Different circumstances. In this case, it may not be a typical patternmaker."

"In any case, it is a remarkable coincidence. Unfortunately, Hamal may have a point."

"Fine. *Three* men in three days, which heightens the threat considerably." Colbis watched Cale, apparently waiting for some sort of sign from him, and when Cale nodded, Colbis raised his voice and addressed one of the guards at the door: "I want a headcount every half hour, and none of my men is to leave the palace grounds by himself. Make it known."

The soldier bowed his head and left.

Colbis turned to Hamal. "The king assigned you to me. Do you understand what that means? I may do with you as I see fit. Under normal conditions, you would go through six months of training and not be out of my sight for weeks, but these are not normal conditions, and Cale seems to trust you. Therefore, to Cale you will go." His voice hardened. "This will be your *only* task while in service to the king. Do you understand me?" He pointed at Cale, saying sternly to Hamal, "You will keep this man alive, no matter the circumstances. He is going to find me a patternmaker, and you are going to make certain he is in the physical condition to do so. Do you understand?"

Hamal didn't know why the captain kept asking him if he understood. He nodded. "Yes." And then, when he remembered, he added, "Sir."

Six hours later, Hamal was standing in his very own bedroom at Cale's house. It had everything he could ever need and more: a real bed, a dresser with a water basin, three windows with real curtains, a table and chairs, and even a closet where he could put extra clothes. And the closet had hooks where he could hang things! He was very excited about the hooks. They were so practical.

Satha watched him with a secretive smile on her face. "Are you pleased with your new quarters, Hamal?"

"Oh, yes," he replied. "It's been years since I had my own room."

"Didn't you have your own room when you worked with Richart?"

"Well, yes, but it was sort of his office."

Her forehead wrinkled a tiny bit. "You slept *in* his office?"

Hamal shrugged. He'd had his own bed and a table and a lamp.

He hadn't needed anything else, and he had wished for those items several times since going to live with the flamemakers in South Barrow. Well, he hadn't wished much for the lamp. Flamemakers were sort of *like* lamps.

"Richart and I often worked until late in the night. It was easier for me to sleep in his office. And he always made sure I was safe there. There was always a guard at the door."

"I'm sure there was. Where did Richart sleep?"

"In his rooms, of course. With his wife. I am very impressed with this closet, Satha. I like the closet." He fingered one of the hooks.

She laughed once. "I believe you would be pleased with anything you were given, Hamal—even a bed in an office with a guard at the door."

He looked at her and grinned.

Her smile grew sweeter. "Hamal, dear, I am glad you were assigned to my husband, and I know that you will keep him safe. Do you know how I know this?"

"Because you are a seer," he replied.

"I know it because you have already proven yourself. You are giving and caring. How is it that you are seventeen years old, yet you have a heart that is more like a father than that of a boy?"

Hamal rubbed the top of his head. A father? He wasn't old enough to be a father. Was she wanting to know how old he was? "I'm not good with numbers," he answered truthfully, and she laughed again.

"Oh, Hamal," she said.

She looked at him solemnly for a moment, and he could feel her gaze the way he felt Cale's.

"I think," she said at last, "that sometimes, saving one person is a greater act than saving many. I think every story in history comes down to the salvation of one person, who then goes out and helps stop the evil that threatens the kingdom. You, Hamal, are a man who saves kingdoms. Perhaps not publically. Perhaps very few people see you as a savior, but the ones you save—we know what you truly are."

She called him a man, not a boy. Hamal shrugged awkwardly, wondering if she was just speaking her thoughts or if she was *seeing* things already. He was just getting used to Cale and his eyes. What would a female seer be like? "I just don't like death," he said. Thinking of her eyes, he said, "And I hate disease."

She smiled. "So do I."

11 The Man in The Tree

Hamal quickly learned what it meant to be a bodyguard. Really, there was only one rule: Everything Cale did, Hamal was expected to do as well. They ate their meals together. They left the house together. Every meeting Cale had with the king, Captain Colbis, or anybody else—Hamal was there, too. Hamal's room was right across the hall from Cale's, and the servants actually woke Hamal up before they woke up Cale.

Cale didn't treat Hamal like a servant, though Hamal was certain that servitude was his real position. A bodyguard was *like* a servant, wasn't he? But Cale didn't seem to think so. It didn't matter where they were or with whom they were meeting; Cale would ask Hamal questions as if he were a natural part of the group, and Hamal would try to give intelligent-sounding replies.

It had been a long time since Hamal had had a good friend. Not since Richart. He liked Cale immensely.

Five nights after Hamal moved into Cale's house, the king came to dinner. He was Satha's cousin, and she explained to Hamal that it was expected for him to visit every few weeks while she was in town.

"Now, Hamal, what do you think of the king?" she asked.

Hamal rubbed the top of his head and thought about his answer. Satha was the king's cousin, so he wanted to choose his words carefully. He replied, "I think he's a very serious man. I know he's a grower, but he isn't *like* a grower. Most growers talk more and frown a little less, I think."

Satha smiled. "Yes, well, think of what you would be like if you were the king. You wouldn't smile very much either, would you? The occupation is a difficult one."

Hamal supposed that was true.

When the king arrived that evening, Satha took her time joining them in the drawing room. When she finally came sweeping in, Cedrick dropped his glass of wine all over the carpet and never noticed.

"By the gods!" he exclaimed. "What happened?"

She smiled serenely and kissed his cheek as if he were an older brother. "Hamal is a talented healer," she replied, keeping her hand on the king's shoulder.

"This is…Hamal's work? Your eyes?" He stammered and said things that didn't make sense and at last managed, "Satha, you are lovely."

She patted his shoulder. "Thank you, cousin."

"And you're a seer. I say, no wonder you and Cale always find so much to talk about."

"No wonder," she agreed politely.

Hamal waited for them to tell the king they were married, but they never did. Not exactly. Toward the end of the evening, Satha reached over and put her hand on Cale's where it lay on the table. A light touch. It didn't seem significant to Hamal at all, except for the fact that it lasted. She kept her hand on Cale's for the rest of the evening, and the king didn't say a word about it. Neither did she, and Cedrick left looking amiable.

"Well," Satha said as the large double doors closed behind the king and his guards, "that went smoothly."

"If you mean that he didn't threaten to kill me, then I agree," Cale answered.

"He wouldn't threaten to kill you, my heart."

"Not verbally."

"Does this mean you told him?" Hamal asked, confused.

Cale smiled at him briefly and then turned his attention to his wife. "No," he replied, touching her bare arm with two of his fingers. "It means that we reached a happy compromise and simply gave warning."

Satha looked at her husband with warm silver eyes. "It means, Hamal, that when he does learn the truth, he will not react with quite as much violence as he might have otherwise."

Hamal realized he was rubbing the top of his head and made his hand lower. He didn't think he would ever be able to predict the practices of North Barrow. They were truly strange.

Shortly after the king's departure, a servant ran into the room through a rear door. Hamal could hear his heartbeat, and he knew long before the man spoke that something had scared him.

"My lord!" The man bowed hurriedly. His face was flushed, his eyes wide. "In the garden! There is a dead man in the garden."

Cale looked tired. In this moment, he looked old, too—much older than his twenty-five years. Hamal felt very sorry as Cale's men cut down the body that had been hung from the limb of a large oak tree behind Cale's home.

"Is it Walkins?" Cale asked slowly.

"Aye," came the answer, and Cale sighed.

The captain of Cale's private guard seemed to be in a state of shock. He kept quietly repeating, "The tree was empty. The tree was empty. I was looking straight at it. Nothing was there."

"It is not your fault," Cale eventually told him, and the calm words seemed to knock the captain out of the bleak hole in his thoughts. The man straightened up and closed his mouth.

The guards carefully laid the body in the snow, and Hamal heard Cale's sigh again. He imagined that any death among his men would affect Cale in a similar fashion. In silence, the seer studied the body. He looked up at the tree, his silver gaze moving across the limb where the man had been hanging, the rest of the bare branches, the trunk; then it moved to the closest portion of the high stone wall that surrounded his property.

"Report," he murmured to his captain, the word quiet.

"The tree was empty," the captain began, then frowned at himself and began a second time: "Normal patrol. No signs of commotion or foul play. Nothing out of the ordinary. Then Ellis gives a shout, and the rest of us suddenly see the body. No one came over the wall. The tree was empty. And then it…wasn't."

Cale nodded, saying nothing more until he looked at Hamal, his gaze intense. "Tell me about the body."

Hamal got down on his knees in the snow beside the body and laid his hand on the man's chest. On all counts but one, he found what he expected to find. The man had died by hanging. His neck was broken. There were bruises on his arms, shoulders, and hands—defensive wounds. He had fought his attackers.

Five minutes.

That was the one thing Hamal had not expected.

The man was hanged five minutes ago. That was all. The neck had been broken for a very short time.

"Oh," Hamal said in surprise. "Cale, what is the man's name again?"

Cale blinked at him. "Walkins," he supplied.

With certain injuries, Hamal found it helpful to speak to the patient and soothe him. Neck injuries were firmly in that category; for some reason, they tended to make people alarmed and could cause long-term difficulty if they weren't handled well in the beginning.

"Hello, Walkins," he said as he began his work. "My name is Hamal. I am a healer, and you know, you should always pay attention when a healer tells you there is no reason to be nervous." He put his hands on the man's neck and then repeated himself, just in case: "Don't be nervous. I'm just going to fix this here and—"

He jerked his hands, and the neck snapped back into place with a loud *crack*. Hamal had heard such noises before, so it didn't bother him. He was actually a little surprised when one of Cale's soldiers doubled over and threw up on the snow.

"—put you back together again," Hamal finished. "There. The worst is over. I can tell you're a very brave man. Well done and all that." He returned one hand to the man's chest and put the other to the man's forehead. A neck injury meant damage to tissue throughout the body, but most of the damage would be found in the brain. It didn't take him long to fix what had been injured; he had repaired physical injuries to brains many times. The main goal now was getting the man to breathe again.

"Hello again, Walkins. It's me. I'm going to hit you now. It might *not* be important to give you advance warning, because I'm not sure you'll remember. But still." Making a fist with his right hand, he brought it down as hard as he could on the stomach, just under the ribs. Beneath his left hand, he felt the chest begin to expand on its own. Once. Twice. Turning his head, he listened closely and began to hear the heartbeat. As he waited, the pulse slowly grew stronger. "Oh, there you are. Good job, Walkins. You made it easy for me. You're going to be just fine. You can sleep it off and you'll be good."

Hamal stood up and brushed his hands off, looking at Cale. "So…he's fine. He was attacked, but he fought back. Lots of bruises on his body. Defensive wounds. I don't know anything more than that, but he'll be able to answer your questions—tomorrow, probably."

The garden was eerily quiet. It was so quiet that Hamal could hear the heartbeat of every man present. He pulled his coat a little tighter.

"Hamal," Cale said momentarily. His voice sounded strained. "Did you just bring a dead man back to life?"

Hamal laughed once. "No, I fixed what was broken. You have to talk to patients with neck injuries. If you don't talk to them, they develop neuroses. They get jumpy and nervous, like spooked horses, and they stay that way for years. I don't know why." He shrugged. "But if you talk to them during the process, they stay themselves and keep calm. Walkins will be fine."

"Can we move him indoors?"

"Of course."

Three soldiers stepped forward to carry the unconscious man inside the house.

The evening was wintery and dark. The last of the sunlight had faded long ago, and overhead the sky was filled with stars.

"Hamal," Cale said again.

"Yes, Cale?"

"I have never seen anyone do what you just did. Was it difficult?"

Cale always wanted to know if things were difficult. Hamal shrugged. "Not any more than anything else. Is it difficult for you to see things, Cale?"

The man blinked at him once and then again. A smile bent the corner of his mouth. "No."

"It isn't difficult to heal either. It is just what I can do. Why did a bad man kill one of your servants?"

Cale straightened, looking at him intently. Hamal laughingly thought that if Cale had dog ears, they would be sticking straight up. "You said the man wasn't dead."

"He *was* dead. It just didn't end in death. There is a difference, you know." Hamal pointed at him. "*You* were dead. Those bad men killed you, but it didn't end in death. It is the same situation. Why did the bad men kill your servant?"

Cale watched him a moment more and then looked back to the oak tree where the body had been hanging. "They used a thiever, probably a man from Dasken, considering the level of talent involved. They captured Walkins, and then it was the thiever who hanged him, willing the body to be seen after he was...was dead, I suppose. Whatever you wish to call it." Turning back to Hamal, he said, "You make as much sense as a thiever in the king's court, Hamal." His voice rose in strength. "Either something is dead or it isn't. Either you are raising the dead, or you're not."

It was, by far, the most emotion Hamal had ever seen Cale produce, and he found he really liked it. With Cale, it was almost funny, though he couldn't have said why, and he grinned and replied, "Both are true! He *was* dead, and I am *not* raising the dead." Cale's men who remained in the garden watched Hamal as he chuckled at their master.

"They cannot both be true, Hamal."

"But they are."

Cale's brows drew together, thick lines deepening between them. "Is it all an act, Hamal—this gullible, overly simplistic mind you present to the world? It cannot be true. You cannot possibly be exactly what you present."

"Well, I don't know. I have a question."

"Yes?"

"What does *gullible* mean?"

Cale hissed a word Hamal doubted he said very often and then tried to compose himself. He drew a deep breath, held it, glanced at his captain. "Fine," he said, sounding calm again. "Act as you will. I don't know why you are doing this. I don't know why you insist on this path, and I won't believe it is true. I do not believe you are as simple as you pretend to be. You can fool others. But you will not fool me." He held his breath again. "And yet I will let you tell me anything you wish, because I trust you. I would listen to a hundred lies."

"Ha," Hamal said, feeling successful, for he had caught him in the joke. "If I ever lied to you, you would know it. You would *see* it. I don't tell lies, but if I ever did, I wouldn't pick you to hear them."

Humor trickled through Cale's metallic gaze. "But, Hamal, that's precisely my point. I *can* see the lie. I can see that you are more than you are acting. I can't see how. I can't see what. But I can see that the more exists. You don't need to engage in pretense with me."

Hamal didn't know what to do with that, so he eventually shrugged and rubbed the top of his head, wishing for a hat. "I wouldn't lie to you, Cale. You are my friend."

Cale studied him. The silver eyes blinked slowly. "I believe that, too."

"Do you know why they killed your servant?"

Cale looked at him a moment longer and then sighed. "They know I..." He paused and started again. "They know that *you* and I have been assigned to the case. By attacking my man, I think they were trying to send a message. They mean for us to be afraid."

Hamal was a healer from South Barrow—a poor man. He didn't understand the signs and signals of North Barrow, where the rich people lived. "A message? What does a dead servant mean?"

"Oh, the usual, no doubt. *Stay away. We'll kill others. Leave this case alone.* Typical messages."

"But he didn't stay dead," Hamal said. "They didn't send a very good message if the man didn't even stay dead."

Cale began to smile. "No, they didn't. What else do you know about Walkins, Hamal? Tell me everything. Are there any details you haven't told me?"

Hamal thought about it and finally repeated, "He has a lot of bruises."

He didn't see how that would be important, but Cale seemed interested. "If he fought his attackers, that means he saw their faces. That's good, Hamal. He may be able to tell us more when he awakens." He turned to the captain. "I want a full guard on him. Walkins is not to be left alone."

"You can put him in my room," Hamal said and shrugged uncomfortably when everyone looked at him. "I mean, if you want to. I can keep an eye on him."

Cale nodded slowly. "Very well. Put him in Hamal's room. And double the outer guard."

12 The Artist and The Angry Man

The servant named Walkins woke the next morning at ten. He was still a little groggy—that could happen with neck injuries— but he was able to answer every question Cale put to him.

Yes, he remembered what had happened. He had been heading toward South Street to pick up a package for Cale's steward, and three men had attacked him not two blocks from Cale's estate. He had tried to fight them off, but apparently, he hadn't been successful.

No, he did not remember the hanging. His face paled at the question. "The *hanging*, my lord?"

From the chair beside the bed, Cale told the poor fellow how they had found him. They had cut him down, and Hamal had healed his neck. To Hamal's relief, Cale didn't say anything about bringing anyone back from the dead.

"No, I...I don't remember that at all." Walkins' brows rose and he added hesitantly, "I don't remember anything except the fight in the alley."

"Three men, you said?" Cale asked.

"Yes."

"And you remember their faces?"

Walkins had already answered these questions. "Yes."

Cale stood up. "Have you ever worked with an artist, Walkins?"

The servant paled again. "You mean…an actual artist, my lord? With the gift?"

"Yes."

Walkins swallowed. "I saw one once, my lord. At a carnival. But I haven't ever worked with one."

Standing behind the chair, Cale put his hands on the back of it and leaned forward in a movement that seemed more like that of a healer than a seer. As a healer, Hamal knew compassion when he saw it. "His name is Jald. I've worked with him before, Walkins, and I trust him, to an extent. He is a gentleman, not a rogue like you'd expect to find at a carnival. The process won't be difficult for you."

Walkins hesitated. Red stole across his face, and he nodded. "Yes, my lord. Thank you."

Out in the hall, Hamal nearly stepped on Cale's heels in his haste to catch up with him. "Cale."

"Yes?"

"I knew an artist once and I liked him. His name was Bill, and he drew with different types of pencils."

Cale glanced at him. "You said the same thing about a prophet."

Hamal grinned. "I never met any prophets who drew with pencils."

A sound scraped up the back of Cale's throat. It might have been a laugh. It might have been a groan.

"I like artists. I'm glad you like them, too."

Cale explained, "Jald works by contract for the king. We send for him when necessary, and he does the best portrait work I've ever seen. Good artists are difficult to come by, and unfortunately, many can be what Walkins thinks of them—burglars and pick-pockets working carnivals. When did you meet Bill?"

"A few years ago. I forget when. It was in Brannack, and he lived in a house on Dolmin Street. He liked pencils mostly, but sometimes he worked with wood, too, and once he dropped a large piece of oak right on his hand." Hamal slapped his right fist with his left palm to demonstrate the wound. "I healed him, and we were friends afterward, though I don't think he really liked me much before. He used to frown at me a lot and say he wouldn't touch me if someone paid him a bag of the king's gold. Something about rocks and thorns in my brain. I don't know what he was talking about. He never did any portraits for me, but I used to go to his house for tea."

Cale smiled slowly. "I don't think Jald drinks anything but wine."

Hamal nodded. "Artists seem to like wine."

"It's true."

Jald looked like the pencils of his trade. From the side, he was the same size the whole way down, and he had the longest fingers Hamal had ever seen. He tried not to stare at them.

"So this is our boy, hmm?" Jald said, staring at Walkins, who went as white as a cloud in autumn.

While waiting for the artist to arrive, Walkins had taken to pacing back and forth across the carpeted floor of Cale's study, but now he stared at Jald and shivered. Poor fellow.

"What's your name, boy?" Jald demanded.

"Walkins, sir."

"What sort of name is that?"

"I was named after my grandfather, sir."

"Well, let's make him proud, shall we? Have a seat." Jald motioned to the nearest couch.

Walkins swallowed hard and sat down, drawing his hands stiffly into his lap. Jald shuffled over to him, and Walkins' eyes grew as wide as candlesticks.

"You can relax, you know," Jald told him.

"I know, sir." The man didn't relax.

Jald sighed heavily. "It will be much easier for me if you just relax."

"I'm relaxed, sir."

"You are not. You're like a cat about to be tossed in water."

Cale caught Hamal's attention across the room and nodded toward Walkins. So Hamal ambled over to the couch and sat down beside the man.

"Hello, Walkins," Hamal said. "Might I have your hand please?"

"What?"

"Your hand."

Walkins' gaze flicked to Cale, who nodded. Hamal could hear the frantic pace of Walkins' heart as the man lifted his clenched hand and forced it open, offering it to him. Hamal smiled encouragingly and wrapped his fingers around Walkins'.

"Artists really aren't that scary," he told the man confidentially. "They just like to drink things. I don't think it matters what the liquid is, as long as it is a liquid. Some like tea. Some like wine. And I once heard a story about an artist who liked to drink milk. That's all he ever drank, and every night he dreamed about cows. What sort of man dreams about cows? Not a bad one, I tell you. Not a bad man."

He waited, watching Walkins' face.

"I like cows," Walkins said.

There it was. "I like cows, too." Hamal nodded. "I should have been a grower."

Walkins thought that was amusing. He laughed harder than a normal man would and, after a while, glanced down at his hand gripped in Hamal's. "What did you do to me, Hamal?"

Hamal smiled. "I relaxed you."

"By the gods, I believe you did."

He didn't even notice when Jald dropped one of those huge, spider-fingered hands on his head and went to work.

Artists and seers were like cousins at the same reunion. The abilities were similar, but seers didn't need to touch anyone for their gift to function, while artists could touch a man and somehow touch his mind. People said that a good artist could see anything he wanted to see in another man's mind—and then find a way to take it. Not every artist was a jewel thief; Hamal knew that, but he had heard the stories, and so he understood how the artist gift could make a fellow nervous.

The better the artist, the better his drawing hand.

"You are looking for three men, you said?" Jald asked Cale.

"Yes. The attack occurred late last night."

Jald muttered beneath his breath, and he kept it up for several minutes. Perhaps it was all the wine, because Hamal didn't catch a word, nor did he remember his old friend Bill muttering like this. Finally, Jald released Walkins' head and sat down at the table that had been brought in for the occasion.

Hamal let go of Walkins' hand.

"I say, Hamal," the servant said. "How long are you going to be staying with us, anyway? I think you should stay for a…definitely for a long time." His eyes were glazed. He swayed on the couch.

"Deep breaths, Walkins," Hamal told him.

"I'm breathing," Walkins replied.

"*Deeper* breaths."

Jald sat at the table and sketched for an hour. At the end of it, he had three portraits that were so clear and precise that Hamal half-expected them to move. Jald, apparently, would make an excellent jewel thief. Three faces. Three men who were working for an enemy.

Walkins confirmed the sketches and then was dismissed. He

staggered from the room as happy as a man could be.

"What did you do to him?" Cale asked.

"I relaxed him."

"Well, yes, I can see that. But what did you *do* to him?"

Hamal chuckled and said, "Have you ever seen somebody who's swallowed too much verdan?" Verdan was a plant that could relieve pain. It had tiny yellow flowers that smelled like dirty feet, but if there wasn't a healer nearby and you needed to feel better, choking down some verdan would help.

"Yes."

Hamal nodded. "That's sort of what I did to him. Not the exact thing, but something similar. He'll be fine in an hour or so."

Pausing as he put away his pencils and other materials, Jald looked at Hamal with renewed interest.

"He works for me," Cale said. "And no, he doesn't make house calls."

Jald muttered some more and then thrust the sketches into Cale's hands. "I'm impressed. That is all. I'm not *interested* in his skills." He sniffed. "I'm reformed, Cale."

A corner of Cale's mouth twitched. "Trying to reform, possibly."

Jald's chin went up. "I believe it is the same thing. Now, if you would have my payment delivered to my sister's house as usual, I would be most obliged."

"Of course. Thank you, Jald. You did fine work."

"Yes, I did. I always do, despite your rude comments about my drinking habits. Hamal, it was very good to meet you." He paused. "If you get tired of being instructed by a seer, do look me up."

The artist left.

"Why does he want his payment delivered to his sister's house?" Hamal asked.

"She is his bookkeeper and his banker. Drinking is not his only vice," Cale answered absently, his silver gaze on the pictures. He arranged them on the table and leaned close to stare down at them. Hamal took a place beside him and looked at the black-and-white images.

One man was older than the other two, and his nose had been broken at least three times. Hamal could count the ridges in the bone. The man in the middle picture had a long, narrow face, and part of his left ear was missing. It was possible that he'd had an earring once, and it had been ripped out. The man in the third picture was the youngest, and Hamal stopped moving when he saw his eyes. They were as hard as steel, and Hamal, who had seen many things, began to wonder what a man as young as this had experienced to make him so angry.

Cale tapped the last image, the one of the angry man. "Hamal, do you recognize him?"

Hamal looked at Cale quickly. "Recognize him? No. Why?"

His voice quiet, Cale said, "I took a ride in a coach with him recently. He was quite skilled with a hammer."

Hamal drew a deep breath. Cale's hand. The hand Hamal could not fully repair. "It was...very dark that night. And it was snowing."

"I remember."

They studied the images in silence, and Hamal's gaze kept being drawn back to the third portrait. He didn't really want to look at it, but he couldn't seem to help himself. The eyes in the picture were angry. So very angry. He didn't think this man was safe.

"Is one of these men a thiever?" Hamal asked. A thiever had hanged Walkins' body in the oak tree. Thievers could make an object appear and disappear. They could change what a person thought he was seeing.

"It is possible," Cale answered, "but I don't think so. Talented thievers usually study their surroundings and want to be familiar with an area before they make a strike, so I don't think they would attack a servant in the middle of the street. It is more likely that the thiever is someone else."

Hamal looked at Cale with delight. "How do you know so many things?"

Meeting his gaze with a sideways glance, Cale smiled slightly and replied, "You've met my man Hurden."

"The man with the limp."

"Yes." Cale nodded. "He's a thiever."

"You have a *thiever* who works for you?"

"I make a habit of having every gift on my staff, or available by contract, at all times, Hamal. It is the only wise thing to do when you are in the king's pay."

"Hmm." Hamal thought of a good joke. Rolling it about in his mind, he picked the best words and finally said, "Do you have a reader?"

"Yes."

"And a charter?"

Cale's silver eyes began to crinkle at the corners. "Of course."

"What about an earthmaker?"

Cale frowned. "What?"

Hamal grinned. He laughed to himself and went back to studying the pictures. He didn't want to look at the angry man anymore, so he purposefully studied the man with the broken nose instead.

After a moment, Cale said, "There is no such gift as an earthmaker."

Hamal snorted. "Cale, you are missing someone on your staff."

The silver eyes probed him. Hamal could feel their push on the side of his face and tried to keep from chortling.

"Why," Cale said, "are you telling me this?"

Hamal shrugged, his cheeks starting to hurt from holding a smile for so long. "I just wanted to point out that you were missing someone."

"Let's say—for a moment—that I believe you are being serious. What does an earthmaker do?"

"He's like a grower, except that he can grow more than plants."

"A grower who can grow more than plants?"

"Yes. He works the earth; his hands are always dirty because he touches the soil, and he makes things grow from it, like stones and birds and things."

Cale turned and faced him, giving Hamal his full attention. "Hamal, I have never heard of an earthmaker before."

"Yes. I think most of them are dead."

Cale blinked at him. "What?"

"I think most earthmakers are dead. Died off. That's why my joke was so funny. You probably wouldn't be able to find an earthmaker to be on your staff."

Cale stared at him. Hamal couldn't help but notice that Cale wasn't laughing.

"Hamal," Cale began, "I am going to ask you this one time. I want you to be truthful with me."

Why did Cale always think he was lying? It hurt Hamal's feelings, because they were friends. They weren't just *supposed to be* friends. They actually were friends. "I am always truthful with you, Cale."

"Well…yes. If you tell me you are being truthful, then I believe you. Here is my question." The seer paused. "How old are you?"

"That's your question? That's easy. I'm seventeen."

Cale leaned forward. "How do you know?"

"Well, that's easy, too. My bones told me."

"Your bones told you."

"Yes." Rocking back on his heels, Hamal said, "I know that you are twenty-five because your bones told me. That night I found you—your bones told me then."

Cale's silver eyes closed, opened again. "I am twenty-five." He sounded calmer now.

Hamal nodded. "I know. Bones never lie."

Cale looked at him a moment more and then returned his attention to the pictures. "I know you don't lie to me, Hamal. I trust you. It is just that sometimes, I think you have a view of the world that is very different than my own."

13 The Second Arrow

Cale had copies made of the portraits. Hamal didn't know where the copies were supposed to go, but they were given to a group of couriers who scattered in all directions the moment they were out the front gate.

In the early afternoon, Cale received a summons from the king, and shortly after the king's messenger left, Cale pulled Hamal aside.

"Something is going to happen, Hamal. On our way to the palace."

Hamal looked up at him, startled. "What do you mean? Did you see something?"

Cale's expression was stiff and *dark* in a way, and somehow Hamal knew that Cale hadn't told him everything. The seer knew more than he was saying. "Cale, what is it? What is going to happen?"

"Just keep your head up," Cale finished.

Cale had never given Hamal a warning quite like this one. Hamal didn't know what to expect. He just hoped he would be the kind of bodyguard Captain Colbis wanted him to be.

The attack happened two blocks away from the palace's main gate.

As it began, the coach stopped abruptly. Hamal had to grab the door to keep his balance. He heard people shouting out on the street but couldn't tell what they were saying.

"Cale, I think you were right." That was what a bodyguard did, wasn't it—warned of trouble when it started? Kept trouble from happening? Hamal had never felt less like a bodyguard than he did in this moment. *I should have had those six months of training*, he thought.

Cale looked at him calmly, as if their roles were reversed and Cale the bodyguard. "Brace yourself." That was all he had time to say.

Hamal didn't even see the arrow. He saw a slight twitch in the curtain over the window, as if someone out on the street had brushed against the coach, and then he heard the beat of Cale's heart change. His head jerked around to see blood on Cale's tunic, just to the left of the breastbone.

"Archer," Cale murmured through clenched teeth.

Hamal could barely hear him above the shouts on the street. *An archer*! People said that archers could find their target even in a crowd. It was possible for them to miss, but this one certainly hadn't. Hamal slid over to Cale's side of the coach.

"Do you want to be awake or asleep?" he asked.

"Awake," Cale replied. "Just get it out."

Hamal put two fingers to Cale's forehead, and the seer's breathing grew easier as he lost his ability to feel pain. A handy trick, that. Take an injured man's ability to feel pain, and he instantly relaxed.

The coach jerked forward, the wheels rolling a single complete rotation, then jarring to a halt. Hamal, fighting for his seat, removed the arrow from Cale's ribs and threw it on the coach's floor. It made his hand sting, and he glanced at the blood on his palm and fingers, then at the arrow on the floor. The arrow was barbed, sort of like a rose stem. His forehead wrinkled. *Why?*

"Archer," Cale said.

Hamal didn't understand why Cale was saying it a second time until fierce heat punctured his back. It felt like a bee sting. Grimacing, Hamal shrugged it away, pushing his fingers against Cale's chest as he healed the seer's wound.

The coach lurched forward. The driver whipped the horses into a run, and it was all Hamal could do to hold on, his hand planted on Cale's chest. He didn't understand something. Cale's blood was reacting to the arrowhead in a way it shouldn't have, and Hamal realized the head had been coated with something. A poison, certainly. The bad men had killed Cale once before, but a sword by itself had fallen short. So they were trying a new method this time. Perhaps that was why the shaft was barbed—maybe the entire arrow was coated in poison. If left in his body, it would certainly kill Cale. And then it would also try to kill whoever removed the arrow. That did not seem very nice.

It took a moment for Hamal to discern the additional elements in Cale's blood and purify the stream. By the time the coach stopped at the king's gate, Cale was whole again, and he was angry.

"Hamal," he said. "We have to get you to a healer."

Hamal twisted around in the seat, reaching for the metal shaft buried beneath his left shoulder blade. It was just beyond his range. He could feel in his own blood what he had felt in Cale's; they had poisoned both arrows, of course. That only made sense.

"I can't reach it," he told Cale. Hopeful, he said, "If you pull it out for me, I promise to be a good patient." It was always more convenient to have arrows removed by friends. Hamal preferred it.

Cale's face grew still as he stared at Hamal. "All right," he answered in a whisper. "If you're certain."

"I would appreciate it."

The gate guards opened the coach's door just in time to see the removal for themselves. Cale had a better hand than he seemed to think he would; he got it on the first try, and immediately, Hamal turned and took the thorny shaft away from him, dropping it on the floor with the first one.

"You'd best let me see your hands."

Wordlessly, Cale shoved his hands forward, palms up, and Hamal cleansed his blood a second time and healed the cuts he had received by forcefully gripping the barbed shaft.

And he talked the entire time. Sometimes it was good to calm a patient down, and in the confined space within the coach, he could hear Cale's heartbeat more clearly than anything out in the court. "Stupid way to kill a man, if you ask me. Arrows. What good does an arrow do? I suppose a well-placed shot could slow a fellow down…but only until his healer gets there, and then what? No more arrow. An easy fix. If you're going to assassinate someone, have a better plan than an arrow."

He realized the guards hadn't waved the coach forward. They were still standing at the door. He glanced at them and the odd looks on their faces and then continued his one-sided conversation.

"I don't know much about poisons. I don't know what these arrows are covered with, but you don't have to know the name of something before you fix it. You'll be fine."

Cale blinked several times, and eventually he, too, saw the guards at the door. "Captain, are we free to continue?"

The captain gave a mumbled order to the driver; the door was shut, and the coach rolled forward into the palace's outer courtyard.

"Hamal," Cale began, "not every healer has your talent. Arrows, in most cases, do much more than slow a man down. You took an arrow for me, and you don't seem to feel it. Explain to me how you did that."

"Well, I took the poison out of you. I purified your blood. And then I—"

Cale blinked. "Hamal, I have seen more than one healer take an arrow for his lord. All of them, without exception, do *not* handle pain well. They can heal pain, but they can't take it very well. You didn't even flinch when I jerked that shaft out of you." He glanced down at the arrows on the floor. "And it was covered with barbs. You noticed the reaction of the guards, I'm sure—they see a wound on a healer, and they know what to expect. But you startled them. How did you alleviate your own pain?"

Hamal shrugged. "The same way I alleviated yours. I don't know why you are asking me about this. It's a little thing."

The silver eyes narrowed. "Do you think you could teach this *little thing* to other healers?"

The coach rocked as it stopped at the second gate that led into the main courtyard.

The driver called down to the guards.

The door opened, and someone shot Cale through the eye.

The seer's head snapped back, his body thrown against the back of the seat. Hamal saw a flash of sunlight on a crossbow and cried out as the first quarrel caught him in the chest. The second gouged his cheek and spread fire through his skin. His vision blurred. He blinked and found himself leaning against the opposite door, one hand on the bench, one hand on the window. The quarrel, from such a close range—

He could hear Cale's heartbeat. It was slowing. The second arrow had penetrated his brain.

He had to save Cale.

All Hamal's thoughts blended to a single point of light that focused on that one intention. That was his only mission while he was in service to the king. Keeping one man alive. One man, so he could save the kingdom. All he had to do was save one man.

And so, he did what Richart had told him never to do within sight of the palace. "Don't let them know, Hamal," Richart had said. "Don't let them see it."

Some things were more important than caution.

Hamal lifted his hand, and he did not heal.

The man with the crossbow toppled just outside the coach, the weapon bouncing on the ground where it fell from his hand. Hamal didn't know who the bad men were and who the good were—they were all supposed to be the king's men—so he did not heal any of them. Every man within thirty paces dropped like a stone.

Surprised shouts arose from the first gate. Hamal heard pounding boots. Running feet. People were coming. *Not yet. Be careful*, he thought.

Wincing, he reached for the door latch. His hands were shaking, but at last he managed to grasp the latch and jerk the door open. He tumbled out of the coach onto the ground.

Men shouted. He heard angry voices. His legs trembled as he tried to stand up straight, which he found to be more difficult than necessary. He had been badly injured. The crossbow quarrel jutted two inches out of his breastbone. That was not healthy. His heart shuddered behind his ribs.

"Hold there!" a soldier yelled.

Taking deep breaths, Hamal scanned the bodies lying on the ground around the coach. There was the crossbowman who had shot him, his form motionless. But where was the archer? Where was the man who had shot Cale in the eye? None of these men at his feet held bows.

The blood thundered in Hamal's body. His vision darkened. Soldiers were screaming orders, and it was growing more and more difficult to concentrate. He lifted his hand again, and all shouts cut off as the company rushing toward the coach collapsed. Hamal didn't look at the soldiers he had just felled. They weren't the ones he wanted—they would be fine.

Where are you? Archers didn't need to be close to their targets. They had excellent aim, even at a great distance. Hamal lifted his gaze and looked across the courtyard toward the palace walls.

Movement near the side door in the palace caught his eye, and just as he turned to look, an arrow slammed into his chest, ripping him off his feet. He fell against the coach.

There you are. His back braced against the coach, he jerked up his hands, both of them this time, and sixty paces away, the archer stumbled and fell headlong.

The courtyard was quiet.

There were bodies everywhere.

Hamal staggered back into the coach. He put a quivering, bloody hand on Cale's leg, to sense the state of the seer's body. Cale was no longer breathing. There was no sound from his heart.

Hamal coughed and realized he was going to need to heal himself first. Wrapping his hand around the stub of the quarrel, he worked it from his chest and healed the wound. He did the same with the arrow, which took a little longer because the head was buried deep. It had stopped somewhere under his shoulder. The scratch on his face still burned, but that was just a nuisance.

He wiped the blood away with his sleeve and sat beside Cale's body on the seat.

"Cale," he said and reached for the arrow sticking out of the man's skull. "If you are listening, this may feel a little odd."

Hamal removed the arrow.

14 Our Mutual Friend

Cale was Hamal's responsibility, his charge, so he pulled a chair beside the bed and waited for him to wake up. Severe brain injuries sometimes left the patient asleep for days, even though all harm had been repaired and the dangers had passed. Hamal could only speculate as to why. Richart would have been able to explain it. Richart had known about things.

Captain Colbis lined the room with heavily armed men who glared a lot. Most of them were big and scary, and Hamal appreciated their presence. Someone bad had tried to kill Cale twice. It was good to give him guards—more guards than just a healer. And this was only a *bedroom* in the king's palace. More men waited out in the attached sitting room.

"They aren't for Cale," Colbis stated, his voice as dry as sand.

Hamal sighed. "I was only doing what you told me."

"I am fairly certain I did *not* tell you to attack my men."

"I didn't know who the bad ones were and who the good ones were—I told you. And I didn't attack them. It was only a temporary paralysis, and I made them all better. Even the bad ones."

"Who are now counting their toes in the king's prison. This is true." Colbis frowned. "I suppose I could thank you. But I'm not going to. In all seriousness, Hamal, no more pretense." He pointed at the bed situated between them. "Cale thinks you are a healer. You work for me as a healer, protecting him. But I have never heard of the healing gift being offensive. I will ask you again, and I will use very small words—how is it that you did what you did today in the courtyard?"

Hamal shrugged and made a face. "I was only doing what you told me."

Colbis' voice grew tense. "I did not tell you to attack anyone."

"I didn't attack anyone! I paused the threat."

The captain's brows began a slow march up his forehead. "You *paused* the threat?"

"If you're trying to attack someone, you're trying to hurt him. I wasn't trying to hurt anybody."

Colbis considered. "That's your logic?"

"Those are my thoughts."

"Do you know what the word *logic* means?"

"Yes. I think so. Mostly."

The captain grunted. "Lovely." He sat back on the couch with a long, drawn-out sigh and frowned at Hamal over Cale's unconscious form. "What am I to tell the king, Hamal? He wants to know how a simple healer incapacitated an entire division. Sixty men, mind you. In a blink. The entire gate patrol. That's an act of treason, you know—leaving a gate to the palace unprotected."

Hamal didn't know what all the fuss was about. Most of those men were back on their feet in less than two minutes. "It is my job to protect Cale. You told me to do my job, and so I did."

"Most healers heal. They don't *cause* disease."

"A temporary paralysis," Hamal reminded him. "It wasn't a disease. I would never give someone a disease. I am a healer."

Quiet fell through the room. Hamal could hear the heartbeats of dozens of men, more than he could count quickly. Colbis had filled the room with soldiers.

"Could you do it again?" Colbis asked finally.

"Of course I could do it again. The king gave me a job. I have a real job now." Hamal nodded toward the bed. "This is my real job. And he is my friend. I will do my job well. And I will use wisdom."

Colbis stared at him. Another sigh blew through the captain's nose, and he said quietly, "I will speak to the king on your behalf. It is possible he will understand and not press charges against you." A noise scraped the back of his throat. "Considering the circumstances."

There was a knock on the door leading from the sitting room, and at the captain's answering call, the door opened, revealing a familiar face. Hamal grinned.

She was as lovely as ever. She had joked once to Hamal that the palace wanted to turn her into an old maid, but it hadn't done anything of the sort.

The captain rose from the couch immediately. "Lady Evalinda," he said, bowing. "An unexpected honor this is. I didn't realize... you and his lordship were well acquainted."

The woman looked at the captain with frosty eyes. Hamal had seen this look many times before, and he started laughing, because it was perfect. Everything he remembered.

Colbis looked at him with alarm.

"I didn't come to see Cale Lehman," the woman answered, the words as cold as her look. She had always managed to look like a queen, even when they were children and Hamal was getting her in trouble with the pigs out in the garden. No wonder her father had been able to find her work in the palace. The palace fit who she was; she was a true lady.

Hamal stood from the chair. "Leelah," he greeted.

The cold in her gaze shattered like a layer of ice on a pool. "Hamal," she replied, suddenly happy and smiling—that also was what he remembered. Oh, the tongue-lashings she used to give people! But she was always warm with her friends.

He walked around the bed and took her hands, standing on his tiptoes to kiss the cheek she offered him. She was tall like her father, while Hamal lived on the balls of his feet. She had warm hands, too. Healers always had warm hands.

"You still need stilts, I see," she teased.

"Kissing you is like kissing a man," Hamal retorted, and she laughed loudly, because she had heard it all before.

She gripped his hands and completely ignored the captain, who gaped from the other side of the bed. "How *are* you, Hamal? We just arrived this evening, and the first thing we hear is that a healer dropped a division in the courtyard with nothing but a raised hand." She frowned at him reprovingly.

He tried to pull away, but she wouldn't let him. "Nothing to be done about it, Leelah. I wouldn't have done it, except I couldn't see any other way. I have another job now, my first job, since your..." He glanced at the captain, whose mouth was still open. "Well, since the death of our mutual friend..." He nodded toward Cale sleeping on the bed. "I am his guard now. I keep him safe. It is a very important job to me."

She sniffed and gave the man on the bed a cold, narrow-eyed stare. "Do you like him?"

"Yes. Very much."

"You think he is a good man?"

"Oh, yes, he is. You can trust him, Leelah. He has a good heart. Like your...our mutual friend."

She rolled her beautiful eyes. "Everyone *knows*, Hamal. And if they don't *know*, they suspect. A jeweler and his wife suddenly produce a healer?" She gave an unladylike snort. "They all know my mother was unfaithful; they just don't know the particulars.

But I suppose if I'm to be your friend, they'll figure out the particulars sufficiently."

"You always were smarter than me," Hamal answered happily.

She laughed at him. "I don't know about that, but I will accept the compliment in the way it was intended. Now—when did you meet your seer? This was the second attempt on his life, was it not? I heard about another attempt in South Barrow. Didn't he nearly die then, too?"

Hamal told her the details, and she finally let him have his hands back, which was good, because he used them as he talked. Hands always made a story better. After a while, Captain Colbis silently stepped from the room, and Leelah moved to the couch where he had been sitting, folding her hands in her lap.

"So now you've come to work for the king," she mused. From time to time, she looked toward Cale as if deciding whether or not Hamal's report about him was true.

"Yes, and I like it. I am happy to have work again."

"Where did you go after Richart's death?"

Hamal shrugged. "To South Barrow. I couldn't find work anywhere in North Barrow. I didn't really have work in South Barrow either. I just volunteered at the mission."

Her eyes grew compassionate. She had healer eyes. "He did that to you on purpose, you know, Hamal, but he did it with the best of intentions. He wanted to keep you a secret. As long as you were held in secret, you could work with him and be happy, and the king would never seek you out."

Hamal nodded slowly. Richart had done only good things, so her explanation wasn't necessary. "But I work for the king now. Are you upset, Leelah?"

This time, she was the one who shrugged. "No, Hamal. I'm not *upset*. Palace life is just very different than working for another healer." Her eyes lowered. "There are so few people to trust."

Hamal brightened. "But you can trust Cale. He told me not to trust anyone in the palace either, and I told him that I could trust you, but he didn't know who you were, and I told him you were a healer who worked at the palace. Where have you been all this time, and what have you been doing, if he has no idea who you are? Richart said he found you work here."

Her head went back, and she laughed uproariously. "A job. How quaint. What a little liar Richart was, but you could never fault him for it, because he would say, 'I have your best intentions at heart. It's all for you, anyway.' And it really was."

Hamal laughed, because he remembered him saying that on several occasions.

"He didn't find me a *job*, Hamal, dear. He found me a husband. I married the governor of Brannack, and I've been living in Brannack for the past seven years. It's a good life, I suppose. Holdan treats me well, and I don't mind telling you that I think I'm in love a little bit. Sometimes he looks at me and I feel it in my knees. How peculiar is that? If I weren't a healer, I would think something wrong with me." She giggled, and her face flushed prettily, and Hamal agreed that she must be at least a little in love.

She looked at the bed again. "If you tell me to trust this fellow, then I will. Moreover, I will tell *Holdan* to trust him, and then Cale the seer will have more work than he knows what to do with. Are you happy with him, Hamal? If you are, then I will leave it alone, but if you aren't happy, I will bring you on with my husband. You can work for the governor instead of the king. You might like it better."

"I am happy with Cale."

She waved her hand. "Fine. Just let me know if you change your mind. The seer was right in what he told you about palace life, Hamal. It can be difficult. After your little escapade today, I believe you will find it more difficult than ever." For the first time, she acknowledged the guards, but she acknowledged them with a scowl, and a scowl from Leelah could be quite frightening.

"But are *you* happy, Leelah? With your home and your husband, the governor? Are you lonely for friends?" Hamal asked.

She hesitated, but as he watched, the rose color crept back through her face, and she breathed a happy little sigh. "Yes, I think I am happy. And you know I despaired of ever being happy in life, Hamal. You remember how we talked about this—I thought I should be quite angry and upset for all my days."

He smiled. "I remember."

"Yes," she said again. "I am happy." She looked at the bed. "How long will he sleep? He looks well." She slid off the couch and went to the bed, setting her hand on Cale's chest. Her eyes grew vacant as she checked the state of his body.

"I don't know," Hamal replied and shrugged. "Head wounds are difficult to predict."

"By the gods," she muttered and withdrew her hand. "You did a marvelous job restoring him."

Hamal grinned. A compliment from Richart's daughter was not to be wasted. "There would have been a scar—you know I always leave scars, Leelah—but one of the other healers helped me."

"Marvelous," she repeated.

"Well, he's my friend. I had to do very good work for a friend."

She looked at him a moment across the bed. A corner of her mouth quirked. "It is good to see you again, Hamal. It is good to see you haven't changed. At all, in fact." Her sharp gaze rolled over him. The quirk in her lips grew more pronounced. "How did you celebrate your eighteenth birthday?"

He made a face at her. "I am seventeen, Leelah. You never believe me."

Her mouth tipped in a smile, and she looked over at the guards and their stoic expressions.

The room grew quiet. There were heartbeats Hamal could count.

She turned back to Hamal. "Perhaps," she said, "some things are better left as secrets."

He smiled and felt very mysterious as he agreed with her. "Perhaps."

15 The Secret and The Sage

Cale slept through the night. During that time, his unconscious form was visited by his wife, King Cedrick, and Captain Colbis, who came every few hours, almost like a concerned mother. The captain gradually reduced the number of guards until only ten remained, but they were ten of the big ones, and no matter what the captain said, Hamal pretended they were there for Cale. Their presence would certainly help Cale, no matter who they were actually supposed to be watching.

Hamal had expected Satha to look in on Cale. After all, he was her husband and she loved him. He expected Colbis, too, because as gruff as he could be, he seemed to be a gentleman, and he wanted Cale to help him with the case. Hamal even expected the king because seers were rare, and Cedrick seemed to be fond of Cale.

The one face Hamal hadn't expected to see was Masly's.

The seer managed to time his visit so that Hamal was mostly alone. Colbis had gone away, and the ten guards who remained didn't seem to see any harm in letting another seer into the bedroom.

As the door opened, Hamal stood out of his chair. "Masly," he said in surprise, forgetting to give a proper greeting. "What are you doing here?" Forgetting propriety altogether, apparently.

Masly's silver gaze went to Cale on the bed. It was just a touch, a brief look to be certain the man still slept. Then he came into the room all the way and shut the door. Fixing his gaze on Hamal, he ignored the guards along the walls. Hamal was beginning to understand that rich people ignored servants and guards. It was as if most of the hired help were invisible.

"Why are you here?" Masly asked.

Hamal had forgotten about the man's squeaky voice. He sounded like he was trying to speak in falsetto on purpose, but Hamal didn't think he was.

"I work here," Hamal answered slowly.

"But why are you here?"

Hamal began to sense that he was missing something in the question. He said again, "Working. This is my work. I keep Cale safe."

"Why did you choose him?" Masly's chin jutted toward the bed. That was how he pointed—with his chin.

Hamal looked at Masly for a moment, trying to decide what the man wanted. It was clear he wanted something—he was acting in a very peculiar way. And this was Masly, the seer Cale didn't trust.

"It wasn't my decision," Hamal said at last. "I didn't choose him. The bad men chose him for me. They threw him out of a coach right in front of me. Of course I was going to heal him."

"So you believe in fate," Masly said bitterly.

"Fate?" Hamal repeated and nearly rubbed his head again. "Why fate?"

Masly straightened, staring at him. "So…you *don't* think it was fate?"

Hamal knew he could be a little slow, but this was ridiculous.

Why was Masly talking about fate? Hamal had no idea what was going on, so he said carefully, "The bad men thought they had killed him. I saw that he could be saved—so I saved him. Sometimes that's all you have to do, you know. You see the good that could be done and so you do it. You just do it." He concluded, "It isn't fate."

The room fell to quiet. Hamal could feel Masly's gaze in a new way, a different way. It prodded at him like a poker that had just been removed from the flames. When Masly looked away, Hamal actually had to adjust his footing.

Masly looked at the guards. "Wait for us in the sitting room."

And they did, to Hamal's surprise. They obeyed just because Masly was a seer. They filed out the door without hesitation, and the last man closed it behind him.

Hamal still felt confused, but he found himself watching Masly with curiosity. Cale didn't trust this man, and he didn't think he was a good man, and so what did Masly want? Hamal really couldn't guess.

The seer folded his arms and stared at Hamal across the room. "I know a reader named Abbart," Masly began. "He works for a wealthy merchant in East Barrow."

Readers were one of the smartest gifts, or so Hamal thought. They were called *readers* because they could remember every word they saw in print, even years later. It was really quite remarkable. Many of them worked as copyists, duplicating manuscripts for businesses and wealthy people. Some worked in the Court of Justice; they were able to remember a defendant's testimony and the accusation against him word for word.

But then Masly continued. "He is interested in the different gifts, and, understandably, your name came up in our conversation this morning." The silver eyes grimaced. "It is quite possible every person in King's Barrow is speaking your name today. Abbart acquainted me with a gift I was not familiar with. It is an old gift, one that has almost passed from memory because the gift is…rather simple. The *nature* of the gift seems to change from person to person; no two men with this gift are alike. However, in each case certain elements remain the same. The common man doesn't even recognize the gift anymore. Abbart called you a *sage*."

"I like the word *healer* better," Hamal said.

Masly stared at him. "You are simply going to admit it without argument?"

This man was strange. Was that why Cale didn't trust him—because Masly was strange? As gently as he could, because he was starting to wonder if he should feel sorry for Masly, Hamal said, "There is no reason I should argue with you, because I agree with you. But I like the word *healer* better. I am a healer. That is what I do."

"You are not a healer. You are something called a sage."

"But I can heal, so I call myself a healer. And people know what a healer is." Hamal laughed once. "If I went around calling myself a sage, people would look at me funny and think I was telling a story." He nodded. "It's just better if I say *healer*."

A few moments passed in silence.

Masly finally said, "Sages are known for their wisdom, but it often does not look like wisdom. In fact, some people think they are fools."

Hamal grinned. "Well," he said and shrugged. "I've never tried to find work because of my brain."

Masly did not laugh. Instead, his eyebrows bunched together in a firm line. "Most sages live quiet lives away from cities. They meet people, form attachments with them, and then stay with them for as long as they can. They don't often marry, and they don't ever become well known." The silver gaze grew sharp. "Most do *not* form attachments with the wealthy, find themselves employment under the king, and save a man's life in the middle of the king's court. They don't want that sort of attention."

"Not a man's life," Hamal corrected. "Cale's life. This is Cale."

"Your attachment," Masly said.

Hamal shrugged. *Attachment* sounded like a big word. *Friend* was much easier to spell.

Masly's gaze dropped to the bed. He was quiet for a time, and Hamal heard the slow, steady increase in the beat of his heart. "Cale used to captain the bodyguard for the prince, Cedrick's younger brother. But three months ago, the prince died on Cale's watch. They were ambushed outside Brannack." The heartbeat jumped again. His soft voice drew close to a whisper: "He thinks it was my doing, that I was involved."

"You didn't kill the prince," Hamal said.

Masly's head snapped up and he looked at Hamal.

"Why don't you just tell him so?" Hamal asked. "You're a seer. He's a seer. You could be friends." It was simple.

Masly rubbed his hand over his mouth and said, "I think Abbart is right. You must be a sage."

"I like the word *healer*," Hamal repeated, and this time he saw a faint smile go across the seer's mouth.

"How," Masly said, "do you know that I did not arrange the prince's death?"

"Your bones told me."

Masly's brows rose. "Excuse me?"

"That first day I met you. Strong amounts of guilt make a man unhealthy in his body. It makes him sick. Your bones told me that you are sick, but it isn't a sickness I can heal—you feel guilty about something. You feel so much guilt that you feel sick." Hamal touched his chest. "On the inside."

Masly just looked at him. There was no emotion on the seer's face at all, but he seemed to be listening.

"There are different types of guilt," Hamal continued, nodding.

"One is guilt because you did something. Another is guilt because you *think* you did something. You—" He pointed at Masly. "—only *think* you did something. Your bones hurt, but there isn't anything anybody can do to heal you. It isn't a healer you need. You need to believe the truth. That is the only thing that can get false guilt out of the bones."

Masly took a slow step backward and lifted a hand. "Hamal, I am here to talk about *you.*"

Hamal waited.

The hand lowered. "I could ask you about your parents. I could ask you where you were born and how old you are." His metallic eyes glinted. "I can see that something is unique about your age, but I'm not going to ask you those questions. For the moment, the most important thing I wish to know is why you are here."

"I don't understand the question," Hamal answered.

Masly nodded, as if he had expected as much. "Sages do not live in cities. They prefer country barrows, where there are more trees and cows than people. But you lived with Richart for years, and then you moved over to South Barrow and lived with the poor, and now you think you want to stay with Cale. Your kind doesn't typically choose the city, yet you have chosen it more than once. Why are you here?"

Hamal shrugged. He felt like he shrugged a lot around Masly. "I want to stay."

"Why?"

"Because I can do some good."

Masly took a step forward, peering at him closely. "Did… Richart tell you that?"

Hamal shook his head. No, Richart hadn't said it, but it would have been like Richart to say it. Richart had cared for the city and done what he could to make it a better place. He had cared for Hamal. They had been friends.

"But someone told you that. Someone you cared for."

"It is good to do good." Hamal smiled as he heard himself speak those words. They were like a rhyme. *Good to do good.*

Masly frowned again. "So your goal, the entirety of your life plan, is to help people."

Hamal nodded. That sounded like a good plan to him.

"And you decided this because someone once told you that it was good to help people."

Did Masly *want* an answer or was he just talking? He didn't seem to be asking a question, yet it felt like a question, so Hamal shrugged again.

"Hamal, you make simple things sound like wisdom, which is a true credit to your gift."

"I just talk and things come out," Hamal replied.

Masly smiled. He had a good smile, Hamal thought. It made his face nicer to look at, and you almost forgot about the squeaky voice.

"That, too," Masly agreed.

He stared at Hamal hard for a moment that stretched on and on and eventually made Hamal begin to squirm. Masly's gaze grew intense, and his heartbeat tripped into a sprint.

Hamal waited.

"It may not have taken a lengthy amount of time...yet it was very difficult for me to come to this decision," Masly whispered.

What decision? But Hamal didn't ask. Masly clearly was upset.

"Seers have different levels of gifting," Masly went on. "It is similar to any other gift. Each seer is unique in strength and ability. That is a reason, a significant *reason*, I made the decision I did."

Hamal didn't know much about the talent of seer. Maybe in *some* ways Masly was better than others, but he could not be better in all ways. Cale was amazing, and he was much braver than Masly was.

Masly wet his lips and said, "Therefore, I have a question for you. It is based on what I have seen. You have wisdom that does not always appear as wisdom. Yet wisdom it is."

Again, Hamal waited.

A flush spilled through the seer's face, and he asked quietly, "If I were to ask wisdom for advice, what would he say? What would you suggest I do about…about the guilt in my bones?"

Hamal startled. Cale had *told* him this would happen. In the Kladis Tunnel Cale had said that Hamal would tell seers what to do. *It is all very awkward, isn't it?* Hamal thought. Telling people what to do was awkward. But in this case, he had a good answer.

"I am a healer," Hamal reminded Masly, "so I want you to be better. I want you to feel good, and I want you to be made whole."

Masly's lips went into a tight line, and he did not respond.

16 The Trial of Masly Hawl

Seven hours later, Cale awoke slowly, blinking in the lamp-light. Hamal slid to the edge of the chair and smiled down at him.

"Good morning," he said warmly. "Except that it's evening. You slept for more than a day, and many things happened while your eyes were closed."

Cale pushed himself up into a sitting position and rested again as soon as he reached it, his back bent, his hands loose in his lap. He couldn't be in pain, but Hamal pushed out of the chair and put his fingers to the seer's forehead all the same.

"Are you all right?"

"Yes. I simply…am not where I expected to be."

Hamal nodded. "It can be like that with brain injuries. Sometimes the memory is affected a bit. What is the last thing you remember?"

"You pulled an arrow out of me."

"Yes, but which time?"

Cale looked at him. "What?"

Hamal patted him on the shoulder soothingly. "The bad man hired men to kill you—and they did. They shot you in the eye. But it didn't end in death." Hamal pulled his hand away. "Did you know the king came to see you while you were asleep? He even made a joke about your eyes being different colors now, but they're not. I checked."

Cale wasn't nearly as surprised as Hamal was to learn that the king could make jokes. "A bad man?" the seer repeated. "Who is the bad man, Hamal?"

Hamal flopped back into the chair and answered, "Some man named Alant. I don't know who he is, but Masly said that he wants the throne, and he thinks he has to kill people to do it—not Masly. Masly isn't the one who wants the throne. It is this Alant fellow who wants the throne. It is like a riddle, I think, because it doesn't make sense. Kill people and get the throne? What does that mean?"

Cale stared at him. "What?"

"A riddle," Hamal explained. "It is a story that actually means something else."

"How do you know the riddle?"

"Masly told me."

Cale stilled. "Masly was…here?"

Hamal smiled, pleased. "I told you—you missed many things while your eyes were closed. And you know, you were right, Cale. You told me that seers would do what I said." The thought still caused heat to spread through Hamal's cheeks. He rubbed his face and said, "And that's what Masly did. He came right out and asked me what he should do. So I told him, and he says he's going to do it. You *told* me what would happen, but still, I don't think I've ever been so surprised…"

All the color drained from Cale's face. "Hamal." His voice grew tense. "Hamal, tell me exactly what you told Masly and what he intends to do."

Ten days later as Hamal walked into the Court of Justice with Cale, his mouth dropped open in astonishment. He had seen the king's Great Hall from a distance, but this room was bigger—much bigger. It was large enough to swallow two or three whole streets, with their buildings and shops and houses and everything. The walls were made of black marble and looked sterile, untouched. There were windows, but Hamal, noticing how high up they started, thought that no one inside the building would be able to see anything but sky, and no one outside the building would be able to see anything inside at all.

Or hear anything, he thought. *Maybe that's the point.*

Three-quarters of the room was lined with thick wooden benches, all of which were already filled. As they squeezed into the last empty spaces near the back, Hamal bumped a large man's arm and had to apologize.

"There are so many people here," he whispered to Cale.

"I know," Cale answered.

In the front of the room stood four tall pulpits. Cale had explained that three of them were for the justices—men with the gift, whose word was law in King's Barrow. The other pulpit was for the king, who listened more than judged in most sessions held in this court. The king wasn't always present during trials here, but today, Cale said, they could expect him.

The king would not miss Masly's trial.

"I didn't tell him to do something bad," Hamal repeated as they waited for the officials to appear.

Cale glanced at him. Hamal could feel his gaze. "You believe he is innocent," the seer murmured. "You still believe he had nothing to do with the murder of the king's healers."

Hamal looked at him in surprise. They had discussed this. Why did he wish to discuss it again? "It is not what I believe, Cale. He *is* innocent—about the healers, I mean. His bones say so."

"Hmm," Cale replied and looked forward again.

They had to wait an hour, during which Hamal twitched.

Finally the herald called an announcement, and the doors at the front of the room began to open.

Hamal slid forward on the bench so he could see better. He had met justices before, but it had been several years ago, and as he looked over their faces, he decided he had never seen these particular men. He didn't know them. Justices tended to be friendly people, or so Hamal thought; they asked lots of questions, sometimes about things Hamal had never thought to be all that important.

Masly was brought in through a second side door. Hamal gasped when he saw the iron shackles on his wrists and ankles and the long chains running through the loops. He was shocked again when he realized the four large guards escorting Masly weren't there to keep him safe; they were there to keep him captive. They thought he was bad. Cale thought he was bad, too. Everyone thought Masly was bad.

The guards led Masly to a square area at the base of the pulpits that reminded Hamal of a pigpen. A tall railing ran on three sides.

Assistants flowed through the back doors and delivered mounds of paperwork up the pulpit steps. *Oh, yes.* Hamal remembered now—justices always liked paperwork. They wanted everything to be written down, even during normal conversations. They had written whole *books* during their conversations with Hamal.

Hamal started twitching again. He could sit for hours but never perfectly still. He twitched.

"It's about to begin," Cale finally whispered.

The assistants collected their documents and retreated down the pulpit steps.

One of the justices, a round man with a very red face, leaned forward and stared severely at Masly. In a ringing voice that filled the entire room, the justice said, "You have been charged with treason against the crown."

Hamal shivered at the coldness in his voice. He didn't remember justices sounding this cold.

"We require your full testimony and will know how you plead. State your name and gift for the benefit of the record."

Hamal realized he was holding his breath and made himself start breathing again. How could Masly stand so still when the justice sounded so angry? Masly looked calm. It was a seer sort of calm, Hamal thought; Cale often had a similar look, and Hamal thought it made Masly look wise and intelligent. His expression suggested that he already knew how the court would judge his case. Perhaps he did.

"My name is Masly Hawl." His soft voice floated through the room. "I am a seer in service to the crown of King's Barrow, and according to the rights of the accused, I may request a counselor."

Whispers stirred through the large room.

"Quiet in the seats," one of the other justices commanded, frowning toward the benches. This justice was the only one with a beard. Hamal noticed that detail as the whispers stopped and the bearded justice turned his frown toward Masly. "Fine. But do remember that according to the same rights of the accused, your counselor may be only one of two gifts: a seer or a justice. And there is no seer in this court who will speak for you."

He didn't even look at Cale, who was watching Masly with a frown. The justice gift couldn't see the future, but it could see what was real and what was not real, so it was often a good judge of men's hearts.

Masly smiled slightly. The motion reminded Hamal of an angry dog that was just about to show his fangs. It was remarkable, actually, how much Masly could make a smile look like a snarl. "Forgive me," Masly said smoothly, "but according to the Panels of Justice, to which this court faithfully adheres, there is a third gift on that list. Any man convicted of any crime has the right to call on wisdom's counsel. Your excellency, I request a sage."

Again whispers filled the room, but this time Hamal barely heard them. A sage? By the gods and everything the gods had made, *why* would Masly want Hamal to help him? Hamal had tried to help him once, and *this* was where it had brought them—to the Court of Justice. This was not what Hamal had been thinking when he had tried to help Masly get rid of the pain in his bones. Why did Masly want to talk to him a second time?

"Quiet!" the justice barked at the benches, and the room silenced. "Masly, do not try the patience of this gracious court. You are fully aware that this court has not seen the presence of a sage in nearly two centuries."

The third justice—a man with perfectly white hair that stood straight up on his scalp—spoke for the first time since the session began. "You are a seer. Why do you make a simpleton's request?"

Hamal cringed on the inside. The justices truly didn't like Masly, did they? Hamal had never met an unkind justice before today.

But this time, Masly didn't make any snarling faces. Instead, he replied quietly, "Perhaps a simpleton is what I should be, your excellency." He sounded like he believed the words.

The chains shifted with clinks and clatters as Masly turned in the prisoner's box and looked through the crowd until his silver gaze collided with Hamal's. He nodded to him and then turned back to the pulpits. "If it pleases this court, I would like to call on a man already in the king's service. Your excellencies, I request that Hamal come to the stand to serve as my counselor. If he is willing."

By this point, Hamal had collected the eyes of every person in the room, and the gaze he felt most severely was Cale's. The weight of his piercing stare lasted for a long moment, and then Cale blinked another of his slow blinks and started laughing. Hamal had no idea why.

"I don't know what to do," Hamal whispered to him.

The room was dead quiet, and people nearby could hear him. Surprised stares became confused frowns.

"Do you wish to serve as Masly's counselor?" Cale asked. He did not, however, lower his voice as much as Hamal thought appropriate.

"Well, last time I tried to help him, he got arrested. So I'm not sure."

Cale was still laughing. His silver eyes twinkled as if he were looking into the sun. "You could have told me that you are a sage, Hamal."

"A healer. I am a healer. I like that word better."

"You aren't seventeen, are you?"

Hamal frowned at him. "Why do you want me to tell you again?"

Cale chuckled like a man who was hearing an old joke he had liked the first time and still enjoyed now. "If you stand as his counselor, you will help him—in a positive way, I mean. I can see it. Should you choose to assist him, all you have to do is stand up and join him in the box. The justices will ask you questions, and you can ask Masly questions; it is a discussion and you will do well. You always do."

Hamal grinned. "You think I always do well? That's very nice of you, Cale."

"Go, Hamal. They're waiting."

Hamal slid off the bench and started walking up the center aisle. Looking around at all the faces, he saw the lords of Kanyan: Mercen the father and Rhyan the son. He saw Leelah, who smiled at him reassuringly, and Captain Colbis. The king stared at him darkly from the farthest pulpit on the left. The justices watched him curiously. Hamal had seen this look from justices before.

The soldiers guarding the prisoner's box stepped aside for

Hamal. He couldn't tell what they were thinking as he walked past, but they seemed to like frowning. Lots of people who worked for the king seemed to like frowning.

"Hello," Hamal greeted Masly.

"Thank you for your help," the seer replied.

Hamal gave him a look. "Are you sure you want my help? Look at you now."

Masly smiled. Once more Hamal thought he looked much nicer when he smiled. It was almost like looking at Masly's younger, friendlier brother instead of Masly. When the seer shrugged, the chains rattled. "Every man needs wisdom. Don't you think?"

"But I never told you to get arrested! What did you do to get arrested?"

Another shrug. Another rattle of chains. "I stole someone."

Whispers filled the air. Hamal laughed, thinking he was joking, and he felt punched in the stomach when he realized Masly was being serious. "You stole someone? You mean, a person?"

Masly nodded amiably. "It is treason against the crown to kidnap a prince."

Hamal tilted his head back and looked up at the king, whose frown had morphed into an intense scowl. "But, Masly," Hamal said. "I didn't tell you to kidnap anyone. Especially not a prince."

Masly's silver eyes blinked. He did not look surprised at the signs of Hamal's concern. "You told me that when you saw someone could be saved, you saved him. Alant has been my friend since boyhood."

"Alant is a prince?" Hamal asked, remembering that Cedrick had two brothers and only one of them was dead.

"Yes. I met him in a closet."

Hamal watched carefully, and when he saw the flicker of humor in Masly's eyes, he dared to chuckle. "A closet? What was he doing in a closet? What were *you* doing in a closet?"

"He was hiding from his nurse. When I found him, he invited me to join in. 'It is good to have a seer on your side,' he whispered. 'That's what my father always says. You have to have a seer to *peer the way* before you.'"

Masly's good humor faded a bit. "*Peer the way.* Those were his words exactly, and I, just a child at the time, felt pleased at my importance. It isn't every day you find a prince hiding in a closet, so I joined him, and I gave warning when the nurse was close. We sneaked down the hallway back to his quarters, laughed at our success, and we've been close friends ever since."

"But I don't understand why you kidnapped him. Is this why your bones are sick, Masly? Because you stole a prince?"

All three justices leaned forward. Hamal noticed the movement and tried not to shiver. They couldn't be *bad* justices. There was no such thing as a *bad* justice.

Masly didn't answer.

"Masly?"

The justice with the bright red face called down, "Hamal, is it?"

"Yes." And again, the manners came afterward. "Um, yes, your excellency."

"And you are a sage."

"I am a healer. I like the word *healer* better."

A moment passed, and then the justice said, "I understand that most sages do prefer to be called by the nature of their specific gift, not by *sage*. Which of your parents was also a sage—your mother or your father?"

"My father."

"What was your mother?"

Hamal smiled. "A healer, of course."

The hard expression shifted as the justice smiled in return. "Of course." Raising his voice, he explained to the court, "Each sage is different, and though the foundational gift of sage remains, the *presentation* of the gift is different in each case." He looked back to Hamal. "Your mother was a healer, and therefore you are a healer. You look like just a boy, but it is my understanding that sages age only to a certain year and then maintain that year for the rest of their lives."

That wasn't true, but the justice didn't give Hamal time to explain. He kept talking. "What year were you born?"

Hamal reached up and rubbed the top of his head. "Well, I'm not very good with numbers."

The justice nodded calmly. "Who was king when you were born?"

"Well." Hamal realized he was still rubbing his head and made himself put his hand down. "Who was the king who built the amphitheater in Riverstone, right on the border of King's Barrow and Theraine?"

The justice's gray brows began to rise. "That was Gracian. He died fifty years ago. That would make you very old, Hamal."

"No, the other amphitheater. The first one."

The gray brows stopped moving.

In the quiet, Hamal went on, "Parve, or Perrave—I can't ever remember his name. But I do remember that he built the amphitheater. He finished it in the spring, and I was just a little boy then, but my father took me to see a play, and I liked it very much. They actually filled the amphitheater with sand, and it looked like a real desert, and my father laughed and told me that when *he* was a boy, Riverstone had been nothing but a desert, and to get anywhere, you had to ride camels. There weren't any buildings or roads or signs that went with the roads, and there weren't any bridges for the river." Hamal perked up. "And dragons lived in Theraine, in the jungles. That has always been interesting to me—there used to be dragons in Theraine. Did you know there used to be dragons in Theraine?"

The justice took a deep breath, held it, then let it out slowly. "Who was king when your father was born?" His voice sounded odd, Hamal thought—a little higher than it had been before.

"Oh, I don't know," Hamal replied. "But you could ask him, if you like. He lives near Jessen Springs. He has a friend there who is a grower, and whenever I visit, I get to sleep in the barn with his horse named Marvel. Isn't that a nice name for a horse? All horses are marvels. But my father doesn't get into town much, so you would have to go find him. The only time I ever saw him in a town was that time he took me to see the play. That was why the king built the amphitheater, you know—so the town of Riverstone would become the city of Riverstone. And it worked. It's a big city now. But King's Barrow is bigger."

Masly quietly cleared his throat, and Hamal remembered they were in the Court of Justice. Here he was telling stories, when Masly was the one with the story to tell.

"I'm sorry, Masly. Enough about me. You go."

A smile twitched the corner of the seer's mouth. "Which part of the story do you want to hear?"

Taking a short step closer to him, Hamal lifted a hand and set it on Masly's chest. He heard intakes of air behind him, but he ignored them, because he was a healer and healers were used to ignoring things. Not finding what he expected to find, he grinned at Masly and said, "I want to know why stealing a man made your bones feel better."

17 The King's Brother

Masly began his story.

"Hamal, to understand what I am about to tell you, you need to realize that Alant is quite mad. He is Landan's firstborn son and the older brother of our king." Masly pointed with his chin toward the pulpit where Cedrick sat in silence, listening.

Masly's voice grew bitter. "I know he's mad. I am his friend, and a seer besides, and I can perceive the madness better than most. He lives in a world that does not exist. He is given to bouts of rage and passion when none can soothe him. He has conversations with invisible men and animals, and he cannot be trusted to function on a daily basis on his own. It was a good decision to pass the throne to his brother Cedrick. No one doubts this ruling—no one wishes to see Alant with authority. You could no more give the throne to a four-year-old and expect him to rule well. I care for Alant like a brother, and I mourn what he could have been. He has greatness within him as surely as madness. I have seen him predict the steps of the king's court long before those steps were actually taken. Despite his disability, he is wise. Too wise, perhaps, for he knows he is mad, and he is capable of using his madness to manipulate the world around him."

The red-faced justice interrupted. "You have been accused of treason, and a clever thing it is to point the story at a man who could neither confirm nor deny it."

"I second your concerns, Ferrick," the king said.

Masly nodded politely. "Forgive me, your majesty. I am merely attempting to tell the story the sage requested."

Ferrick, the red-faced justice, muttered something, and the king frowned at Masly.

Masly continued. "Hamal, Alant is restricted to the north wing of the palace, where his activity is closely monitored. Anyone is welcome to see him; however, he is not permitted to leave the north wing under any circumstances." Masly paused. "Three years ago, Alant sent for me, as he often does, and when I arrived in his quarters, which are as familiar to me as my own, I found him to be in good spirits. He seemed himself, but it was not a true presentation.

"Every time he sends for me, it is for a reason. Perhaps not a good reason. Sometimes, indeed, he wants something ludicrous that does nothing but convince others of his madness. Over the years, he has asked me for many things that I will never give him. He wanted a horse head once. Another time, he asked for a doll with all the arms and legs in a separate bag so he could bury the toy one piece at a time. His humor is dark, and it grows darker as the bent of his mind progresses. He grows worse; he does not improve."

Masly took a slow breath, and Hamal felt that the seer was steadying himself, like a man about to jump off a cliff into deep water.

"This particular time, he said he wanted me to do something for him. Such statements from Alant are difficult to predict. You don't know from moment to moment if the request will be from a more stable mind or from one that is darker and slightly more creative. That day, the request was far from sane. 'I want you to kill a healer for me,' he said. 'A man named Richart.'"

Hamal heard two gasps. One he thought was his own, and the other came from behind him, in Leelah's direction. Richart was her father, though most people in the court didn't know that.

"He wanted you to kill Richart?" Hamal asked, and his heart grieved. Richart had been one of the best men Hamal had ever known. A great man, with a true healer's heart. "Why would a madman locked away in the palace want to kill Richart? Richart was hardly ever at the palace. He didn't like coming here."

Masly's silver eyes narrowed as he studied Hamal. "You aren't going to ask me if I did as he requested? If I killed Richart?"

"Of course you didn't kill Richart. No one here thinks you killed Richart."

Lifting his head, Masly looked up at the justices for a few moments. Eventually he continued his story. "Alant told me that he wanted to be king. In his mind, his father had simply put him at the bottom of the list, as if he were the lastborn. He thought that if he killed his brothers, Landan would have no choice but to make him king. 'If you're going to kill a prince,' Alant said, 'the first thing you have to do is kill his best healer.'"

The courtroom was so quiet that Hamal thought all the heart-beats sounded like the boots of an army.

"He sounded so certain. The request was terrible—a true sign of his madness—but I could see how strongly he was convinced of his path. His confidence turned my stomach, and I attempted to correct his thinking. I told him that his father cared for him and regretted his condition, but he had made his decision. Alant wasn't on the bottom of a list. Even if something happened to his brothers, Landan would never name Alant his heir. Alant's face turned a mask of red rage, and he shouted at me for half an hour. His nurse and the guards came to calm him down, but to no avail. Alant felt that I had issued him a challenge. As I left, he said, 'You'll see, Masly. I will do it with or without your help.' Three months later, Richart was dead, and I *know* Alant was somehow responsible."

The king stirred on the pulpit. Standing below him on the ground, Hamal thought his nose looked longer and sharper than ever. "Alant did not kill Richart," the king said.

"Agreed," Ferrick added.

"But he died," Hamal said quietly, remembering the day they had found his body. The pain was like a bruise on his heel. Sometimes he could forget about it, but then he would accidentally poke it and remember it was there. He carried it always.

The king didn't say anything more.

Masly shook his head once and blew out a frustrated burst of air. "He said he was going to do it, and then it happened. That was…that was the first time. When I told him his father was dead, he grieved, but then he said kings needed to die so princes could become kings in their stead. Then six months ago, he asked me to kill Teiren."

Again, the courtroom dropped into a quiet so deep that Hamal could hear hundreds of heartbeats. He thought *Teiren* was the name of the prince Cale used to protect. The king had only the two brothers.

"I told him no," Masly said. His heartbeat was rapid, like a little child's when he was afraid of a monster in the dark. "Remembering what had happened with Richart, I went and told the king, who increased the guard. Surely, that would be enough. Wouldn't it be enough? Alant couldn't even leave his rooms. He has no power in the city—none. Surely, additional guard would be enough. I visited Alant almost every day to observe, and one afternoon, he laughed and told me he was going to be king soon—and I knew. I saw that he had done something, despite the guards, despite the impossibility. I ran out of his rooms, grabbed the first healer I could find, and went to Brannack, and…" His voice dropped away.

Masly swallowed hard. The silver eyes blinked. "And the only one we managed to save was Cale. Twelve men. Every one of the prince's guards, all of them armed and more than capable. And all of them dead." Masly's face reddened and then slowly turned a grisly shade of white.

In the heavy quiet, Hamal said, "I don't understand, Masly. Why would any of this make you feel guilty?"

Masly answered slowly, "Lately, he's been talking about killing healers again."

Hamal almost turned around and looked at Cale. Alant was killing healers? They had found the two bodies in the river, and while Cale was unconscious, another body had been found buried under some boxes in an alleyway behind one of the temples. Another healer who worked for the king.

But then Masly added, "He has become quite interested in the king's seers as well. One seer in particular."

Hamal took a startled breath. "You mean Cale? He wants to kill Cale, too?"

Masly nodded. "Alant claims to have killed six healers already, and he grows frustrated because he keeps failing with Cale. I can't…I can't listen to such talk anymore, Hamal. I can't be a part of it."

"How are you a part of it?"

Masly's voice dropped into a whisper. "I have tried everything to stop him. I tried."

Hamal started frowning. "But I still don't understand why you would feel guilty. Such strong guilt, too, when you did nothing. You are not responsible for the prince's actions."

Masly didn't seem to hear him. "I can't make him stop. He won't listen to reason. He's become obsessed with killing the king's healers. The first time I met you, Hamal, I tried to steer the king away from you. I could only imagine what Alant would say when he found out about *you*—a talented healer associated with the seer he has tried to kill multiple times. I would be sending you to the wolves."

"*You* would be sending me to the wolves? But, Masly, it isn't your job to take care of me. I can take care of myself."

"I couldn't take it anymore, so when I learned you were a sage...I knew I needed wisdom. You told me to get rid of the guilt, and so I did. I found a way to make sure no one else died. I removed the prince from the palace. Somehow—someone in the palace is working for him. That is the only possibility. Someone is doing as he asks. And I will find out who it is." Masly looked down at the chains on his body. "Or someone will find out. It doesn't matter who, as long as it is done."

"Masly." Hamal put his hands on Masly's shoulders, and the seer finally stopped talking. "Masly, it is not your fault that Alant is behaving this way."

Deep lines appeared between Masly's brows. "I know it is not my fault."

"But it isn't your fault that he killed all those people either. No seer can see everything, just as no healer can heal everything. I can't heal everything—and I always leave scars. You and Cale should be friends I think, because he understands that he is good enough, and you need someone to show you how it's done."

Hamal patted Masly on the shoulder. "You did act with wisdom, Masly, just not the wisdom I meant. Did you take the prince someplace safe?"

A long moment passed before Masly answered quietly, "Yes."

"What do you think we should do to find the bad man who is helping Alant?"

Masly glanced up at the justices, and when none moved to interrupt, he told Hamal, "I think a better question is what you think

I should do now."

"Well." Hamal thought about it. "The king wants his brother back, I suppose?"

They both looked up at the king, who nodded.

"Maybe you could bring the prince back to the palace, and I could put him to sleep."

Masly looked doubtful. "Put him to sleep?"

"Oh, yes—any healer can make a man sleep. I made Cale sleep once." Hamal turned around in the box and waved at his friend, who, after a moment, waved back. Why did Cale turn red so often? Hamal would have to ask him. "See? He's fine. If Alant is asleep, he can't harm anyone, can he? And he can't speak with whoever his bad friend is. Oh! And you know who else we could use? That artist fellow! What's his name? Jall? Jalt? I can't remember, but he can draw people's faces. He could show us everybody who's been to see the prince, and you and Cale could decide who the bad man is."

"Hamal, your plans always seem quite simple," Masly said.

"Yes," Hamal replied and then teased him: "It's part of being wise, you know."

18 What They Found at The Farm

Masly took them to an old farmhouse outside the city. To Hamal's eyes, it looked like every other sprawling farmhouse between the city of King's Barrow and Brannack, and he thought no one would have been able to find the prince without Masly's help. It was a good hiding place. The fields were white with snow from a fresh fall last night, and Hamal wondered what kinds of fruits and vegetables the farmer and his family liked to grow each spring. Most farmers were growers because they liked working the earth so much. They even liked trying to grow things in wintertime. It was likely the barn over there was filled with plants.

"I don't see any guards," Hamal said, shivering. He saw cattle and horses around the barn and men in heavy coats doing farmer things near the house. But not any guards. "Shouldn't there be guards?"

Masly grinned. "Oh, but there are guards. That's the beauty of it. The captain and I will go in and get him, if it pleases you, your majesty."

Hamal watched as Masly and Captain Colbis rode up the drive, the captain holding the reins of an extra horse.

"Hamal," Cale said. His horse stamped an impatient hoof on

the snowy road, and the seer shifted his weight in the saddle. "You may need to…relax the prince for the journey back to town."

"Relax him?" the king asked. Today he wore the clothes of a jeweler, and like the guards who escorted them, he did not look like anyone important. Hamal didn't see a spot of armor on any man in their party, but he did see a lot of swords.

"Hamal's touch can have a cathartic effect, your majesty." Cale paused. "I see that the prince will not be pleased with his companions for the return journey. A little relaxation might be in order."

The king grunted once and returned his brooding attention to the house.

A few minutes later, the front door of the farmhouse opened, and even across the distance, Hamal could hear a series of flamboyant curses, shouted at the top of a man's lungs.

"Oh, my," he murmured, and from the next horse Cale laughed softly.

"We seem to be having a bad day," the king said in a dry voice.

Masly and Colbis returned with the prince, who recognized Cale from a stone's throw away and fell into a dark sort of silence that Hamal thought he could almost feel on his skin. *I prefer the cursing*, he decided right away.

Alant was better looking than his brother. He had a finer nose, but there was something strange about his eyes, something that didn't seem right, and even the horses didn't appreciate his presence. The animals began to toss their heads and nicker at one another, ears laid back as Masly, Colbis, and Alant joined the rest of the party on the road.

Alant glared at his brother and then at Masly and said, "So I am under arrest. I thought as much."

His voice somehow matched his eyes. When the prince spoke, it was as if he stared at you, even when he was looking somewhere else, and Hamal fought off an intense shiver. No wonder no one argued about whether or not Alant was sane. This man was dangerous. Something was wrong with him.

"You are not under arrest," the king replied. He sounded calmer than Hamal felt, and it was clear he was used to his brother's effect on his environment. "We are simply moving you back to the palace for your own safekeeping."

"Safekeeping," Alant repeated. "How I love that word." His face did not look like he loved that word.

Cale caught Hamal's attention, and as the seer nodded toward the prince, Hamal girded up his courage and slid off his horse into the snow. Instantly, the prince's dark, dangerous eyes clapped onto him.

"Who is this?" Alant demanded.

Schooled by Cale, Hamal answered, "I'm a sage. I just want to take a look at you." Cale didn't want him to say his name or that he was a healer. Alant did not like healers, and it was probable he knew Hamal's name.

"A sage." The eyes flicked to Cale then the king. "There is no gift called a sage."

"There is," Hamal replied. "You just haven't heard about it because you've been locked up. May I see your hand please? I'm not going to hurt you." He smiled helpfully and pointed at Alant's boot, armed and at the ready in the stirrup. "You can kick me if I do."

"I don't kick children," the prince muttered.

"Oh, well, that's one good mark for you."

Hamal took Alant's cold hand when it was finally offered, and the first thing he did was try to relax him, which Alant clearly needed.

But it was surprisingly difficult, because all the bones started talking at once.

Before this, Hamal had wondered if he had ever met a case like Alant's, and the moment he touched him, he knew he hadn't. This was new. The bones were louder than they should have been, but the worrisome thing was that they told Hamal only good stories. There was no pain, no guilt, no grief, no events of trauma. According to his bones, Alant had never harmed a soul or made a single bad decision. His bones and his eyes told two different histories.

What are you doing? Hamal asked the bones. It wasn't a real question. He didn't expect the bones to actually give an answer. The situation was just…odd. Bones didn't tell lies. They always told a man's history according to the truth.

Only when he touched the man's blood did Hamal begin to understand.

"Oh, there you are," he murmured.

Out the corner of his eye, he saw Masly and the king straighten in their saddles.

"What is it?" Masly asked.

"What did you find?" the king asked at the same time.

Hearing the concern in their voices, Hamal knew they both loved Alant, despite his many faults. Masly had been the prince's friend since childhood, and Cedrick was Alant's little brother, who had probably adored him growing up, the way little brothers often do. It was good when family and friends loved one another. It was good when they continued to love, even when one person in the group made it difficult.

"Your highness," Hamal said, ignoring the others, "I understand you spent seven days at this farm. Did you enjoy your time here?"

"I'm not an invalid. Do not speak to me in that manner."

Hamal squeezed the hand once, waited a moment, and then repeated the question. "Did you enjoy your time at the farm, your highness?"

"Yes, I did. Anything to get out of the palace. I would take a sewer in Brannack if it meant getting out of the palace."

"I suppose you like pretty snowy fields? And cows?"

"Yes, I like cows. Very peaceful creatures."

Hamal smiled to himself. He liked cows, too.

He finished his work and returned Alant's hand to his thigh, patting it soothingly as he peered up into the man's eyes. "How do you feel now, your highness?"

"What is a sage, exactly? Is that like a plant you would find on a farm? Isn't there a plant called a sage? I feel good, actually. I feel very good. I think I might use the word *very* more often, because it has started to seem quite true to me. I feel *very* good. What is a sage? Why have I never heard of a sage before?"

Hamal stepped back and turned to face Cale and the others. "I think he's calm now."

Masly, staring at his friend the prince, didn't seem to hear Hamal, but Cale and the king gave him their full attention.

"What did you find?" the king repeated.

"Holes in the blood," Hamal replied.

"Holes?" Cale asked.

Hamal explained, "Most people don't have these holes—you don't have them, Cale. But when a person does have them, they can cause him to think things that aren't true. The blood is important. It needs to be healthy, and blood with holes in it is—well, it's blood with holes in it. It can't do what it was made to do because things are missing."

The king traded a look with Cale. "What are you saying?" Cedrick asked. "Did you...somehow restore him?"

Hamal grimaced. "No. No, I can't replace missing pieces. Healers can't do that. It would be like making something from nothing—it would be *creating* something, not healing it. I can't create. I can only heal and sometimes not very well."

Turning around halfway, he lifted his arm and pointed up at Alant's face. Alant didn't seem to mind the attention. At this moment, he probably wouldn't have minded anything. "See his eyes? That look in his eyes is not right, and I can't take that look away. His bones don't register that he did anything bad, because his mind doesn't register that he did bad things. He doesn't see it, and I can't fix what is not physically broken."

Cale nodded slowly. "Did you *ease* his condition? Will his episodes now be less severe?"

"He needs an alchemist, Cale."

"Don't you think we've tried that, Hamal?" Masly asked.

Hamal heard the bitterness in the seer's voice. "Well, a good alchemist can sometimes do what a healer can't, because they can add things to a person's body, and I can only heal. I think Alant will be a little better now, but I am sorry that I can't make him fully well. I've never been able to heal a person's mind. It is like trying to heal a…a piece of sand. Or a rock. It is completely different than the rest of the person. It is out of my realm."

Alant quirked a smile. "Comparing my mind to a piece of sand. Thank you."

Laughter stirred through the guards. It seemed like genuine laughter, too, which surprised Hamal at first, considering the circumstances. But then he remembered how Alant had been able to lead men and tell them what to do even from his fancy prison in the north wing. Men listened to him. Something about him drew them to obey. It was almost as if he were a king, even though he wasn't a king.

Masly urged his horse forward, reining next to Alant stirrup to stirrup, and they began a quiet conversation back and forth. Cale and Cedrick began a quiet conversation of their own, and for a moment, Hamal was left to himself. He took a deep breath of the cold, clean air.

The day was quiet and peaceful, the farm relaxed in a way the city wasn't. Hamal hadn't been on a farm in years, and he had forgotten how pleasant the country could be. Reins in hand, he paused before climbing back into the saddle and looked out across the snow. He thought about visiting his father. Farms always made him think of his father. Jessen Springs, where his father lived, looked a little like this place. It snowed all winter long up in Jessen Springs—sometimes even after the flowers started blooming.

A few minutes later, the king commanded, "Let's get him home," and the group began to turn west, back toward the city.

I really should visit more farms, Hamal thought. *But later, when it's warmer.* Perhaps one day he would live on a farm again.

As he remembered good times, the idea interested him, but he looked over at Cale and smiled to himself and reasoned the farm could wait. Some things were more important than farms...like people. Like a good friend.

19 Next Time

Jald the artist had no desire to put his hands to a madman and said as much using large, angry words. It cost the crown a good deal of money and the settlement of some back taxes to get the artist through Alant's front door and into his sitting room. But the process went smoothly, or as smoothly as could be expected, and at the end of six hours, Jald produced sketches of the five men with whom Alant had spent the most time.

"You can't expect me to make this easy on you," Alant said pleasantly.

"You never make anything easy," Masly replied.

Two of the five men were already in chains in the prison, having been arrested the day they tried to kill Cale in the king's court.

The next day, three of Alant's private guard were arrested for murder and several other charges Hamal couldn't remember. All he knew was that they were supposed to be good men. Only good men were supposed to work for the king, but something had gone wrong. Those three men had been hand chosen by Masly to serve in Alant's private guard, and the seer had been unable to predict their eagerness to appease a prince.

"I don't think I would be happy as a seer," Hamal told Cale one night on their way to the palace.

On the other side of the coach, Cale turned to him with silver eyes. "Why is that?"

"It would be a hard job. Hard things. I think seers must be lonely."

Cale was quiet for a moment. The coach rocked beneath them. Hamal could hear people calling to one another out on the street, and a dog barked somewhere nearby.

"Well, sometimes people surprise you," Cale replied. He released his breath in a sigh. "Tonight, for example, we are going to visit Masly."

Hamal brightened. "Oh, he lives at the palace?"

"Not in the manner you are thinking," Cale wryly replied. "He currently resides in the king's prison."

Hamal's jaw nearly touched his knees. Sliding to the front of his seat, he asked, "Masly is in prison? Why is Masly in prison?"

Cale smiled softly. "He took a member of the king's family out of the palace by force, Hamal. The charge of treason was a true charge."

"I didn't realize he would be arrested again."

"He never stopped being arrested; they never let him go after the trial. He made his choice, and he knew the outcome. The justices actually gave him mercy, something they do but rarely; he could have lost his head. Instead, he is confined to the prison in the southern tower, which happens to be finer than most of the rooms you would find in South Barrow. It is not a harsh sentence against him. Not at all."

Cale folded his hands in his lap and looked out the window. He seemed to be thinking.

For a few minutes, they rode in silence. The street was quiet all around them, but Hamal gradually began to hear music coming from one of the buildings on the right side of the street. It wasn't a house; peering out the coach's window, he thought it looked more like another government building. North Barrow was filled with government buildings. There were many of them on this street in particular, because they were so close to the palace.

Sitting back in his seat, Hamal looked across the coach at his friend Cale. Cale worked for the king—the king liked Cale. And for very good reason. Hamal had never suspected that he would be spending this much time in the palace of King's Barrow. The palace was a very fine place, but it needed Cale. Hamal didn't think he would like it without Cale.

Masly said that Cale was Hamal's *attachment*, but that made him sound like a lady's hand purse. Hamal snickered to himself as he thought about Cale turning into a hand purse. It would have to be silver, of course. A silver purse.

Cale glanced at him. The seer took a deep breath and let it out. "This is not how it will always be, Hamal."

Hamal straightened. "What do you mean?"

"With Masly. The Court of Justice would see him rot in prison, but the king respects him more than they, and I have seen that he will not be there long. It is possible that you and I will need Masly in the future."

Hamal looked at Cale with new excitement, his interest piqued. "How will we need him?"

But Cale only smiled. "You see, Hamal. Being a seer has its benefits."

And he would not say anything more, even though Hamal pestered him relentlessly.

Acknowledgments

No paper child is born without the help of nursemaids. Yes. That is what all of you are—epic nursemaids.

A huge thanks to Brooke Walsh, Cherish Brunner, Jennifer Stapleton, Jane Lambert, Susan Stinton, and Angie Goldberg for helping me with the manuscript. You guys graciously listened to me wax eloquent when I was in the honeymoon stages of writing. I know how I get when I'm writing, but you guys stuck around anyway.

Trace, you have pretty fingers. I mean, you have creative fingers that can make pretty things. As always, thanks for your help with my books! You've done an amazing job.

Carla, you also have pretty fingers. Like Trace's but smaller. Great job with the calligraphy. You help make me look cool.

If you love Hamal,
get more of his story!

Visit

TheHamalbooks.com

Made in the USA
Monee, IL
06 December 2020

51325757R00111